The Wrong Goodbyes

The Wrong Goodbyes

By

S. C. Clements

ReadersMagnet, LLC

The Wrong Goodbyes
Copyright © 2023 by S. C. Clements

Published in the United States of America
ISBN   Paperback: 978-1-960629-66-1
ISBN   Hardback: 978-1-960629-68-5
ISBN   eBook: 978-1-960629-67-8

All rights reserved. No part of this publication may be reproduced, stored in a retrieval system or transmitted in any way by any means, electronic, mechanical, photocopy, recording or otherwise without the prior permission of the author except as provided by USA copyright law.

The opinions expressed by the author are not necessarily those of ReadersMagnet, LLC.

ReadersMagnet, LLC
10620 Treena Street, Suite 230 | San Diego, California, 92131 USA
1.619. 354. 2643 | www.readersmagnet.com

Book design copyright © 2023 by ReadersMagnet, LLC. All rights reserved.

Cover design by Ericka Obando
Interior design by Dorothy Lee

DEDICATION

I dedicate this book to my husband, Rob, who allowed me to spend as much time as I needed writing about my life before I was so fortunate to have met him in my later years and to my loving sister who edited this manuscript.

PREFACE

"Good morning Mrs. Farwell. How are you feeling today?" my nurse Cyndi asked as she was raising the shades of the window in my small room.

"I'm doing as well as expected, I guess. At least I am up and sitting in my chair waiting for breakfast to be delivered. I hope I get pancakes and sausage this morning. I think that has always been my favorite breakfast meal even though I never made it very often," I smiled.

"Why is that ma'am?" she asked while making up my bed.

"Well, like you, I used to be a nurse and for most of my forty-year long career. I worked evenings or nights. I just didn't get up in time to fix any kind of breakfast or I would go straight to bed after getting off duty from being so tired after working the night shift which we called the 'graveyard shift'," I said.

"Wow! I know that feeling. I didn't know you had been a nurse," she answered.

"Yes, I loved my career! I truly believe nursing is a calling from God for most of us who venture into that field of endeavor," I said.

As she looked at me more inquisitively while straightening up my nightstand, she said, "I have a few minutes to spare. I would love to hear about your life."

"That is so kind of you, thanks. You know, when we get old, it often seems like the young folks don't realize we were young once too and had the same worries and challenges that you face today. After we retire and reach a certain age, we are hidden away in little rooms such as this and forgotten about. Sad really. So I do appreciate your interest," I said with a few tears welling up in my eyes.

"Oh, I'm so sorry about that truly, Mrs. Farwell," sharing her concern.

While smoothing out the folds in the blanket laying across my lap, I returned her smile with a wink and began telling her some of my life story as it began when I entered the United States Army Nurse Corps during the Vietnam War era.

CHAPTER ONE

After a restless night's sleep contemplating my decision over and over in my mind, I was awakened by a cool breeze gently brushing across my cheeks as it drifted through the sheer curtains of my bedroom window. The coolness was appreciated because these past few days in June we had sweltering afternoon temperatures. Homes such as our blond brick ranch style built in the late 1950's had no air-conditioning, so all the electric fans were turned on by midmorning and all the draperies drawn by early afternoon.

As I slowly stretched and got out of bed, I noticed I didn't hear any stirrings throughout the house. I did hear the faint sound of the little wooden bird jumping through the door of grandfather's cuckoo clock announcing it was eight o'clock. Mom inherited this coveted clock that he brought from Germany during his youth. It was mounted on the south facing dining room wall. I didn't know until years later that I would be the benefactor and protector of this antique as well. I loved this little clock!

Apparently, dad had already left for work after tending to his flower garden, much admired by all the neighbors. Almost daily before sunrise, he would wander among his flowerbeds of perennials and annuals giving them water and nutrients when needed. Often, he proudly escorted family and friends through this colorful tapestry announcing the names of his numerous roses as if they were his children. Fragrances filling our senses! The little Dutch windmill and pond in the southwest corner of the yard added an extra dimension to this beautiful landscape.

I remember grinning as I walked past his bedroom every night seeing numerous garden magazines strewn about the bed and even partially covering his face while hearing him snore. It always pleased me to see he had finally drifted off to sleep because he would be awakened several times during the night from the sound of the ringing bell coming from across the hall in what used to be the bedroom where my sister and I slept.

A hospital bed had been placed in this bedroom for mom. The proximity to the master bedroom allowed dad to hear the ringing of the bell when mom needed relief from the severe pain that gave her restless nights.

My grandfather had been staying with us for a few months in part because of my mother's serious health condition and in part because it was our turn on the family "merry-go-round" to house him. After grandmother's passing from a severe stroke, he lived with each of his four daughters. My mother, the youngest of six children, was my grandfather's favorite even though it was forbidden to ever say one had a favorite. He always looked forward to coming to Denver, but this visit was bittersweet!

I was sure he was up and either sitting in the living room reading one of his favorite novels, perhaps Herman Melville's "Moby Dick" or possibly taking his daily walk around the neighborhood. Now that he was getting close to eighty, he exercised as much as possible. I would sometimes take a sneak peek through a window just to observe him strolling down the sidewalk past the neighboring homes. I was concerned he might fall, but he always had his cane with him.

His daily ensemble consisted of a stiffly starched white shirt with decorative cufflinks, striped, gray, or black trousers held in place with suspenders, and a gray soft felt fedora hat that covered his silky snowy white hair. He always made sure it was securely positioned so as not to be blown away by any sudden gust of wind. I would laughingly smile thinking he could be the elderly fashion icon for GQ magazine. I didn't think he would do much walking today, however, because of the predicted heat wave.

A fruit bar I placed on top of my bedside table the night before was nourishment enough for me this morning as I needed to finish packing before my 10:00 a.m. departure. I could snack again once I boarded the plane or enjoy a nice meal that airlines offered back in the seventies.

This was a very emotional time for me. I was gathering my thoughts to express my sadness for leaving. But, unfortunately, it did not happen as planned. I heard my mother's voice from her bedroom across the hall just as I finished cramming treasured belongings into my suitcase.

"What you are doing is wrong! You know how much this upsets your father and me."

"Yes mom, we have been over this topic a dozen times. This discussion has exhausted any further solutions," I snapped back as I carried the suitcase into the central hallway, while at the same time trying to dismiss her concerns as well as mine.

Changing the subject, I sadly asked, "Where is grandfather?"

"He doesn't want to say goodbye to you! He is ashamed of your decision too," mom retorted.

That word "ashamed" really resonated. Forgetting mom's comment, I refocused on my fond memories of my grandfather. I loved him so much and it made me sad seeing him standing at the far end of the living room looking out the patio door toward dad's water fountain and flower garden. Why wouldn't grandpa look back at me? He knew it would probably be several months before I could return home. Maybe mom was right, maybe he was ashamed of me.

My thoughts then strayed to our move to Colorado. My brothers and sister and I had to learn to adjust to city life after spending our youth in small towns and living on farms and ranches in Nebraska and South Dakota. We never lived too long in one place as dad always had dreams of greener pastures. But as children we did appreciate his enthusiasm and we experienced many adventures we would not otherwise have had.

One farm, just a mile from our little college town where I was born, had belonged to my other grandfather, a Danish emigrant. My dad planted a row of trees when he was twelve years old as a future windbreak when the trees matured, which they had of course when we lived there. I felt so proud knowing dad had planted this grove as a boy, and now as a six-year-old I could see the care he used to cultivate these beautiful trees so many years ago.

We had the usual menagerie of livestock. The milk cows would slowly walk back to the corral and into the barn every evening for milking when my dad yelled, "Here bossie, here bossie." One of the bulls, a Brahma, frequently exited the corral by jumping off the chute madly running around the driveway with his head down, proudly displaying the large hump on his upper neck and large pointed horns swinging about (a sight to scare anyone). In addition we had sheep and I got to feed a few of the newly born lambs, sadly due to their mother's rejection (the reason unbeknownst to us) and pigs — I was so amazed watching cute pink little piglets with curly short tails being born. Of course, there were chickens and I hated gathering their eggs for fear of being pecked to the point it would puncture my skin and draw blood. The ducks would follow behind me when I came out of our house, waiting for me to feed them a delicious treat of moist oatmeal. There was a two-week-old puppy that I fetched after having been carried in his mother's mouth up the hill behind the house into the "badlands" pasture, where the rattlesnakes and a few cacti lived. This was because our dog "Lady" didn't think he would survive being the runt of the litter. Then there were cats who wandered about the farm feeding on mice and even rats!

Most farms and ranches had bull snakes living in their barns to minimize the rat population. I remember my mother went into our basement to do some laundry and found a bull snake coiled around the water pipes suspended from the ceiling! That vision still makes me cringe!

When we lived in town, I remember we were one of the first families to have a television set because dad owned one of the two hardware stores. That was exciting! Also when he owned a car dealership in a nearby town where we later moved, my brothers and I loved walking across town with our friends after school to his business just to have a tasty bottle of Coca-Cola from the soda machine after begging him for some coins! The drink tasted so good on a hot afternoon!

Dad bought a 7000-acre sheep ranch in South Dakota when I was about four years old. We lived in a "sod house" and when it rained, which seemed rare, we had to position buckets on the floor of every room to collect drops of water leaking down from the roof! One day, I remember being so excited to see my uncle land his biplane in the field across from the house for an afternoon visit after flying up from Nebraska. Most of the neighboring ranches were cattle ranches and having a sheep rancher amongst them was not to their liking. But every rancher along with their wives and children gathered for frequent weekend square dance parties, so we were soon welcomed into the "clan"!

I recall so many interesting stories growing up as a child, thanks to my dad.

I am sure it was difficult for mom to hear we were to be packed up for another move after just getting settled somewhere. Fortunately for us, this move to Denver was our last. Each of us had to make quite an adjustment! The junior high school I was enrolled in had a class size larger than the entire school I attended in our small towns. But, after graduating from high school each of us could pursue our own interests and dreams, even though my dreams and career were impacted by my mother's illness.

Arguing with mom, knowing how seriously ill she was, would haunt me for months. She was almost too weak to leave the hospital bed that dad had rented for her since her surgery, which had been over a year ago. The bed was positioned under the window, so it was difficult to view the outdoors unless she was standing. But mom spent most of her time lying in bed reading her bible when the sedating effect from the pain medication diminished. The outside world did not concern her much now.

Unfortunately, life with Dad was not easy for mom. She often stated that he was not the man she married after he returned from WWII. His new habits of smoking and drinking were of great concern to her. Especially the frequent weekend drinking binges which led to many discussions of divorce. Her new priority was to raise her children to be God loving, honest and hardworking, plus no smoking or drinking was allowed. She didn't want those vices penetrating our souls!

Sadly, I recalled a night when my brother Jim, then a senior in high school, came home quite late after being out with his friends. While lying in bed, I could hear him throwing up in the bathroom. Suddenly I heard mom screaming at him while using "the belt" to whip him as he slowly crawled back to his room. I wanted so much to rescue him. For years neither of us discussed that unfortunate experience.

Despite raising her children with good moral values and reading bible verses to us when we came home from school for lunch each day, mom and I just never got along very well. We seemed to always find something to argue about. I vividly remember her criticizing me during my youth; the hairs of my eyebrows were not aligned; I slouched too much; I was "pigeon-toed"; I was too much of a tomboy; I didn't sit still with my back straight when playing the piano; and the list goes on and on. She enrolled me in a "charm school" I recall when I was a young teenager, so I could learn the graces of how to sit properly and then stand without out falling over while wearing high heel shoes, that I really doubted I would ever wear. I had to learn how a young lady was supposed to enter and exit a vehicle. Proper etiquette while sitting at the dinner table was adhered to as well. She was trying her best to "tame" me.

I felt she was embarrassed having a "plain Jane" daughter. She demonstrated her preference for my older sister so many times during my childhood. I recall running into the bedroom to "cry my eyes out" several times as a small child due to her scorn or scolding. I always hoped my mother would come in and give me a hug and say she loved me, but sadly she never did.

Cynthia was pretty and smart like my mother, who at one point in her youth wanted to be an actress. Both dressed very stylishly and wore only the most expensive clothes, it seemed to me, while accenting their attire with lots of bangles or jewelry.

I on the other hand lived in my brother Jim's light brown faded cotton t-shirt and an old pair of cut off blue jean shorts. At night I would drop them onto the floor beside the bed and put them right back on in the morning. During the warmer months, I went barefoot as well. I just accepted that I was the "ugly duckling" in the family to use the Danish author Hans Christian Andersen's words from one of his fairy tales. But fortunately, as the story goes that little duckling eventually turned into a swan, but not soon enough to erase the damage to my psyche from my mother's neglect.

I remember when I was a student nurse, I was at home fixing my mother's hair one evening and giving her a makeover after her recent surgery. Many of my classmates wanted me to cut and style their hair even though I had no special training, so I felt confident that I could do the same to mom's satisfaction.

Suddenly she said, "Susan, you have so many talents!"

This shocked me since she rarely complimented me. Maybe she remembered that I spent many evenings working on advertising art projects for special events at the hospital, or that I was vice-president of my senior class, or maybe she was thinking of the times I had to drive to an evening modeling assignment. I do know these creative outlets probably provided some emotional and psychological benefit to me.

Knowing I never measured up to her standards during my youth, my immediate reply was, "Mom, it is too late!"

After this flash of memories began to fade, my anxiety returned. I felt a headache coming on. I saw my boyfriend Jeff's convertible parked at the curb in front of the house. I was a little surprised he did not get out and come up to the front door. But knowing my decision to leave home was partly at his suggestion may have been the reason for his reticence.

He met my dad only once along with my brother Gary when he picked me up for our first date. Dad was impressed because Jeff was going to be a doctor, a career my dad pondered before the war, but after serving four years in the Army during WWII that dream ended. Dad had new responsibilities with a wife and a young daughter. He felt four years of medical school plus several years of a residency and possibly a fellowship were unrealistic. This was a decision I think he regretted for many years. He struggled financially with his career choices creating some of the demons he struggled with thereafter. So, it was important to him that I had a life free of financial worry; being married to a physician was a pleasing thought for dad. My intention, however, was to probably never marry. It was not important to me, especially after the experience I encountered with my best friend Kathy's fiancé.

She and I became good friends while taking nursing classes. I was living at home my first two years as she did as well. Living only miles apart we took turns driving to class and often along the way we would review the questions for daily quizzes or exams.

"Okay, Kathy, what is the main gastric enzyme secreted by the stomach?" I asked while turning my head quickly in her direction as I drove down Colorado Boulevard in the red 1966 Buick convertible that dad had purchased for me to drive after high school graduation.

"I know that one! It is pepsinogen, and it is secreted by the gastric chief cells," she proudly stated.

"Very good Kathy! See you can do this. Just take a few deep breaths to help you relax when the test papers are handed out. You know the stuff," I answered trying to offer as much encouragement as I could.

Kathy received high marks on oral exams but was extremely fearful of written exams. Asking her questions as we drove to class did not seem to help. She was upset that I always received the higher grade. But as true friends, she asked me to become Maid of Honor for her upcoming wedding the summer before our final year of school. Not only was I concerned she was too young to marry at the age of nineteen, but I was also certain she picked the wrong man.

One beautiful Saturday afternoon several classmates along with Kathy and I, as well as her fiancé, decided to have a picnic in the city park, just weeks before their marriage. Disturbing to me, it seemed Tim was paying too much attention to me that afternoon to the point that I felt quite uncomfortable and embarrassed for Kathy. Mindless of his amorous gestures towards me, she and the others decided to stroll through the park flower gardens, while I stayed behind to help Tim clean up after lunch. He was sitting on the blanket lighting up a cigarette as I was picking up the dirty paper plates and putting them into a trash bag.

"Hey, I'm free tomorrow night. Why don't you come with me to this new club?" he casually requested while trying to create smoke rings when he exhaled.

I was shocked and disgusted!

"Did I just hear what I think you said? Tim, what is the matter with you? I cannot believe you would even ask such a question, and just weeks before your wedding, my God!" I replied angrily.

"Hey, these are my last few days of freedom. I figure I can do or say what I want. Kathy will never know," he grinned.

I tartly replied, "Oh yes she will, because I plan to tell her!" Suddenly he became silent.

A few days later I did tell Kathy hoping she would cancel her wedding to this despicable guy! Not only did she not cancel her wedding, but she told me I was no longer her Maid of Honor. Since I already had my bridesmaid dress, she consented to let me be one of her six bridesmaids. But it truly sickened me to see them standing side by side before the priest in the church sanctuary repeating their vows to one another. I thought if I ever married, the relationship would be based on trust and honesty. Months later I learned that Kathy was pregnant and possibly that was her reason to dismiss my comments. She probably felt it was too late to stop the marriage and being a Catholic, she did not have many options. Our friendship soon waned. But that was no longer a concern, as I was stepping into a new world now.

Standing in front of the doorway, I did call out to say goodbye to grandpa. Because of his severe hearing loss, I told myself he just didn't hear me, since he never turned around to look my way. I recall he never entered into the discussions I had with mom and dad about my decision to leave home. So, I truly didn't know how he felt about it. I might have been afraid to ask him because I respected his life choices, and if this was a mistake on my part, I didn't want to hear it from him.

I had already embraced mom while she was sitting up in her bed, but emotion was frozen in time somewhere. Cold as that sounds, I did cry many times after she received the diagnosis of cancer. I prayed for God to take me and spare my mom's life. I was nineteen years old then, and my twin brothers were seventeen. I especially felt sadness for them because they were just finishing high school. I thought they were too young to possibly lose their mother.

Walking down the steps, I took one last look at the house, wondering what might change while I was away. I knew dad would take good care of mom as he had since her surgery for the colon cancer. He hired a cook to come in each day to prepare meals for her, even though she really had no appetite. My brother

Gary would help, I assured myself. My sister, Cynthia had moved away to Oregon after recently getting married. My other brother, Jim was in Hawaii stationed in the Navy. He too wanted to get away from home, but for different reasons than mine. His grades were poor while attending his first year of college and he decided he was wasting his tuition money, so he quit. He did not get along well with dad; his decision to leave home was easier for him. Grandfather's stay was poorly timed, but the majority decision was to let him come to our house. I know seeing his youngest daughter wasting away before his eyes was almost too much for him to bear and my leaving was an added sadness.

I recalled how much I loved listening to grandfather's tales of his family coming across the plains in a covered wagon in the mid 1800's. The perils of this journey were numerous. Many died from cholera, typhoid fever, TB, and even smallpox. Fortunately Indian attacks were rare, but three of his siblings had died on that treacherous journey. I was amazed that he survived at the tender age of four. Then when his family arrived in Nebraska where they decided to stay, they had to live in camp tents for long periods of time through all kinds of harsh weather until they found land on which to build a home. In those days a house was much different than what I knew. His home with his parents and older sister consisted of only two rooms with dirt floors! But they were happy to have a "house" and land.

I was truly amazed and actually shocked on hearing him tell about his youth. Thinking back on those precious times I got to spend with him made it so much more painful not giving him that final kiss and hug goodbye. My tears were pouring by this time, as I ran down the driveway to the waiting car.

After opening the passenger door for me, Jeff offered these consoling words, "You made the right decision, Susan. As I told you before, you cannot continue living in your parents' house knowing that your mom may have a year to live, sad as that sounds, while not being able to tell your father, sister, or brothers and even your mom about the inevitable. This is too much for you to bear. I don't understand why Dr. Macrae encumbered you with that responsibility."

As I wiped the tears from my eyes, he continued, "I am going back to New York to see my folks next week and I will fly down to San Antonio to see you as soon as I can. Give me a call when you get there, okay?"

Jeff's words were reassuring, but I do not know how comforting they were. As mom's intern at the time of her surgery, he knew too well what her final days would be like with the suffering. I did as well having taken care of cancer patients myself.

I immediately thought of the first patient I had as a student nurse. He died at the age of nineteen, (my age too at the time) while his parents and I stood closely by his side. He believed he had a promising career ahead of him playing football. He had just started his freshman year at a local university using that football scholarship he worked so hard to receive. He wanted to be the "star" quarterback. Shockingly for him and his parents, the pain in his knee that he thought was just from a football injury turned out to be osteosarcoma, a cancer found in bone forming cells, especially in the joints.

His death was the first I had experienced as a new nurse and there were several more during that year after I graduated. Each one was difficult for me. I could not hold back my emotions as I tried to give care to them and their families. I recall during my nursing classes, we were told to remain calm and almost stoic when dealing with death, but I felt the families and patients needed to see and know that the medical staff had sympathy as well as empathy for them during such sad times.

As these nursing experiences passed through my mind, the hour-long trip to the airport seemed like only minutes. If Jeff was talking to me, I did not hear anything he said. After driving up to the curb near the check-in outside the terminal, he quickly stepped out of the car and gave me a strong hug and kiss. With my ticket in hand, I slowly walked through the sliding glass doors with my suitcase. I felt some comfort knowing I would see him soon.

CHAPTER TWO

As the plane was ascending, I stared out the window at the colorful patterns on the ground below and viewing this beautiful terrain, mitigated my sadful thoughts. I felt some concern about what my future would hold. But, having developed a sense of self-reliance and independence by the age of sixteen, I was somewhat comforted knowing the decisions I had already made were sound, despite the dissent of my parents.

The Vietnam War which started in November of 1954[1] was still active when I decided to join the Army. I thought since my father had been a Captain in the Army during WWII, he would be proud of my decision to enlist. But he was not happy at all. In fact, he contemplated moving to Canada to keep my younger brothers out of this terrible war. His own personal experiences and my naivete provoked many discussions on this subject.

I vaguely remember going down to the recruiting office and raising my right hand to take that oath, "I _____, do solemnly swear that I will support and defend the Constitution of the United States against all enemies, foreign and domestic; that I will bear true faith and allegiance to the same; that I take this obligation freely, without any mental reservation or purpose of evasion; and that I will faithfully discharge the duties of the office on which I am about to enter. So help me God."[2]

I did not feel any remorse for my decision. So often when I was still a nursing student, I watched the evening news (especially

---

1 Ronald H. Spector, "Vietnam War", *Vietnam War/Facts, Summary, Years, Casualties, Combatants, & Facts*, https://www.britannica.com/event/Vietnam-War
2 Oath of Commissioned Officers, *(Title 5 U.S. Code 3331, an individual, except the President, elected or appointed to an office of honor or profit in the civil service or uniformed services)* https://www.army.mil/values/officers.html

on CBS) to listen to Walter Cronkite. Seeing graphic images of the numerous wounded and dying American soldiers being sent home from Vietnam disturbed me greatly. I usually cried after watching this.

I believe the CBS news network was the most viewed broadcast at that time because we trusted Walter Cronkite. At the behest of his Executive Producer, he went to Vietnam to report "on the ground" events. Prior to this, he was considered a "war hawk" and his reporting would be noted as factual and informative for the American people. Sadly, he was troubled by what he witnessed firsthand which contrasted with what then President Lyndon B. Johnson was telling the American public. On February 27, 1968, surprisingly to his audience, he summed up his Special Report from Vietnam: "Who, What, When, Where, Why?" He felt the war was unwinnable and remarkably this war was costing the United States around $25 billion a year![3]

The conflict was between the communist government of North Vietnam and its allies against the government of South Vietnam and its allies, of which The United States was the principal ally. This war was also part of a larger regional conflict known as the "Cold War" between the United States and the Soviet Union.

Our involvement really began in 1961 and troops were sent over to Vietnam in 1965. By 1969, when I became a registered nurse at age the age of twenty, there were over 500,000 military personnel stationed in Vietnam.[4] I remember feeling so sad seeing the staggering number of casualties, and I thought perhaps, being a nurse, my training could be helpful in some way.

That was not the sentiment of some of my friends, however. Many boys, as I will refer to them when I was a senior in high school, were scared to be called up for duty. Conscription or "the draft" was mandatory enlistment into the armed forces. This draft

[3] Walter Cronkite and the Vietnam War, https://blogs.uoregon.edu/frengsi387/files/2014/06/276081_original-
[4] Ronald H. Spector, "Vietnam War, 1954 - 1975", Vietnam War/Facts, Summary, Years, Casualties, Combatants, & Facts, https://www.britannica.com/event/Vietnam-War (2021): 2

was not new to this war. It dated back to the French Revolution of the 1790's and military conscription dated back thousands of years before that. Resistance to being drafted did reach a historic peak during this Vietnam War.[5]

Almost 40,000 young men were sent up to fight each month.[6] Families were afraid of losing their sons. Many recent high school graduates joined communes and/or became conscientious objectors, which meant their religious teachings and moral aversion to war kept them out of the military. Draft cards were burned. Over thirty thousand young men fled to Canada, settling into major cities such as Toronto, Montreal, and Vancouver. They were described as well- educated and supplied a strong workforce for Canada. However, half of them did return to the United States after they were pardoned by President Jimmy Carter in 1977.[7] Other young men married, hoping that having their wives conceive a child would exempt them from military servitude. Steep fines as well as jail time were punishment for running away from this obligation.

The 1976 book "What happened to the Class of '65" by David Wallechinsky and Michael Medved mirrored my own class of '66. I remember one evening I received a call from one of my best friends, Nina.

"Susan, I'm down here at the police station. Cody and I have been arrested along with hundreds of other students!"

"Oh my gosh, Nina!" Why and what can I do to help?" I asked alarmingly.

"It's this damn war! We were protesting the evil promulgated by the news about the death of those students at Kent State! I already called my dad, and I think he will be down here shortly

---

[5] History.com Editors, "The Draft," *History*, https://www.history.com/topics/us-government/conscription (2020) updated from original (2017): 1-2

[6] History.com Editors, "Widespread Disillusionment," *Vietnam War Protests*, https://www.history.com/topics/vietnam-war/vietnam-war-protests (2022) 2

[7] Cori, "Draft dodging in the days of the Vietnam War," *Canadian History, History, Moving to Canada, USA*, https://remoteswap.club/draft-dodging-days-vietnam-war/ (2016) 2

to bail us out. Susan, I am so glad he is a lawyer!" she said with a feeble attempt at laughter.

"Wow! I am so sorry Nina, but fortunately your dad will be there soon to get you out of that place! Is there anything you want me to do?" I asked, while trying not to reveal dismay through my voice.

"No, I think I just wanted to let you know and to hear a friendly calming voice. There is a lot of pandemonium around here right now. I guess the police think we are idiots! God, what's wrong with this world?" she replied with disgust.

On May 4, 1970, Denver University where Nina's fiancé Cody attended had a "sit-in" of about 1500 students mourning the loss of fallen comrades at Kent State University, as did many other colleges and universities around the country.[8] Even though university officials at Kent State tried to diffuse the unrest, the Ohio National Guard opened fire on a crowd gathered to protest the Vietnam War. Four university students were killed and nine were injured. The campus shut down for six weeks after this tragic event.[9]

Many song writers were inspired to compose music regarding this protest about the Vietnam War. Pete Seeger wrote "Bring 'Em Home" in 1966. Marvin Gaye's "What's Going On?" in 1971 became one of the most popular songs of all time. And John Lennon's "Give Peace a Chance" from 1971 extended well beyond that war to present day.[10] "We got to get out of this place" written by Barry Mann and Cynthia Weil was recorded in 1965 by the British group "The Animals". It was frequently requested and played by American Forces Vietnam Network disc jockeys, soon to become the Vietnam anthem.[11] When many of the

---

8   Wikipedia, "Woodstock West," https://en/wilipedia.org/wiki/Woodstock_West (2021)
9   History.com editors, "Kent State Shooting," https://www.history.com/topics/vietnam-war/kent-state-shooting (2020) updated from original (2017)
10 History.com editors, "Vietnam War Protest Songs," https://www.history.com/topics/vietnam-war/vietnam-war-protests (2020) 2
11 Wikipedia, "We Gotta Get Out of This Place," https://en.wikipedia.org>wiki>We_Gotta_Get_Out_of_This_Place (2022)

platoon soldiers had marching drills, they would sing in cadence this song. Great sound really as I listened to these soldiers shout out those lyrics, while at the same time feeling misery at what awaited them in battle. Very sad times for all.

A ceasefire had been called on January 30, 1968, in celebration of a yearly Vietnamese holiday of Tet (the lunar new year). But early in the morning North Vietnam attacked over a hundred cities and outposts in South Vietnam in an attempt to have the United States scale back its involvement in the war. Americans became shocked by these attacks and the massive casualties. This victory by North Vietnam marked a turning point in the war. The "Tet Offensive" was successful in that America began withdrawing troops.[12]

The Pentagon Papers, commissioned in 1967 by Secretary of Defense Robert McNamara, took eighteen months to complete and caused many Americans to question our stake in the Vietnam War. We were becoming weary and untrusting of our government. Subsequently, President Richard Milhous Nixon announced an end to US involvement in January of 1973.[13] The Paris Peace Agreement was signed on January 27, 1973, seven months after I finished my two-year military commitment.

---

[12] History.com editors, "Tet Offensive," https://www.history.com/topics/vietnam-war/tet-offensive (2020) updated from original (2009) 2

[13] Editors of Encyclopaedia Britannica, "Pentagon Papers, United States history," https://www.britannica.com/topic/Pentagon-Papers updated recently by Michael Ray, Editor

CHAPTER THREE

I was not sure if there were other recruits on the plane going to San Antonio, but after landing, without averting my eyes to look for possible familiar faces, I took the escalator down to the baggage claim area one floor below, retrieved my suitcase, and proceeded to the passenger pick-up area. As instructed in my information packet, I waited there for the bus that was to take me, as well as others, to the military Army post. I saw several young adults standing nearby. I assumed they were medical recruits. Maybe one or more of them would become my tiered bunkmates.

I had images of what the barracks might look like since I had seen pictures somewhere; maybe from my brother Jim when he joined the Navy. I was not looking forward to this six-week stay. But I realized I had to go through the required military training "bootcamp" before I could proceed to the school of training in my field of nursing which was OR (operating room nurse). This specialty I soon learned was an extremely critical MOS (Military Occupational Specialty). With the numerous casualties from the war, my skills were greatly appreciated not only in the stateside military hospitals, but especially in the hospitals and MASH (Mobile Army Surgical Hospital) units in Vietnam. So, I assumed I would receive transfer orders for Vietnam after my three month OR course was completed.

As our driver was throwing my suitcase into the storage space below, I stepped up into a musty smelling hot bus, due in part to the humid sweltering city heat, and slowly walked towards the rear. I was hoping to have a seat to myself, but within minutes a girl slightly overweight, with a long blond braid sat down beside me. Soon thereafter, all the seats were filled. Noise and laughter penetrated the thick air.

With a handshake, she immediately said, "Hi, my name's Kelly. What's yours?"

"Susan," I curtly replied, not really wanting to start up a conversation with anyone. But, not wanting to be rude, I continued to let her engage me in chitchat.

"I'm from Mobile, Alabama. "What about you?"

"I thought you sounded like you were from the south with that accent. I flew in from Denver, Colorado," I replied.

She grinned, "Oh, it never occurred to me that I had an accent. This is my first time out of my home state. We all sound alike there, I guess. Gosh, Denver! I would love to see the Rockies, especially in the winter. We don't see much snow in Alabama you know," she winked and paused, saying, "Maybe I can put that on my dream sheet."

This "dream sheet" may have been a fantasy, but recruits could request four duty stations as their desired posts following bootcamp.

Continuing, she added, "I'm a dietician. This will be my first "job" before going out into civilian life. "Civilian life" doesn't that sound strange. Since the Army paid for my college tuition, I owe the government four years of my life. I had to lose forty pounds before I could enlist though. Darn! I sure hope I can keep it off. I don't want to have to buy new uniforms every six months," she nervously laughed. "Are you a dietician too?"

I sensed possible trepidation from her with the battery of questions thrown my way. But I imagined many of us wondered why we made the decision to be here in the first place.

"No, I am a registered nurse and worked a year before deciding to join the Army. I thought I could help in some way," I replied as I slowly turned to look at the passing cars outside while feeling the cool moist breeze entering the open window as we continued to share a little personal information with each other.

About a half hour later, we arrived at Fort Sam Houston. The driver told us to remain on the bus until he returned from reporting our arrival.

"Okay, those of you in the first six rows of seats follow me. The rest of you stay here until I get back," he ordered after bouncing back onto the bus.

Wow! What is that about, Kelly and I wondered as we looked toward each other with raised eyebrows.

Within twenty minutes or more, he returned and after glancing at his watch, he looked up at all of us and immediately said, "It is after 1700 hours now and since we arrived so late, I have bad news to share with the rest of you. The barracks are now full."

I did not know what 1700 hours meant, but the sun was beginning to fade, and I knew it was probably too late for dinner, and the "chow" (military jargon for meal) might not be too tasty anyway. I would learn military time and military terminology in due course. Looking around I sensed most of us were somewhat concerned. Where were we going to eat and sleep, especially tonight since all of us had had a long day of traveling?

He continued, "The good news is that I will transport the rest of you to the San Antonio Inn not far from here. The building was finished just a few months ago, so this beautiful hotel will be your home for the next six weeks, you lucky stiffs!"

We could not believe our ears! I think suddenly we felt a bit superior to the rest of the recruits who had to stay in the Army barracks.

The trip to the hotel seemed short and when we grabbed our luggage, he told us he would see us at 0500 in the parking lot for our ride back to the post for rollcall the next morning and every day after that for our six-week bootcamp. Wow! Why so early, I wondered.

Once the hotel clerk gave us our assigned rooms, she immediately mentioned that this hotel was now segregated. The men were staying in the south corridors and the women were staying in the north corridors. We were not allowed to mingle in the hallways or make any loud noise that might disturb other guests at the hotel.

All of us were medical personnel as I had suspected. Most of the women were nurses along with a few dieticians while the men were dentists and doctors. This career gender division was the norm then. Women felt that fundamentally their only occupational choice other than motherhood was a teacher, a secretary, or a nurse. Professional positions such as a doctor or lawyer were almost exclusively for men. If a woman ventured in those fields of endeavor, that was considered an anomaly, and they were not well received into the clique.

This segregation that we were told to abide lasted only until everyone gathered at the outdoor pool at the end of each day. And we soon realized the rules became more lenient as the weeks passed.

I liked my room on the third floor. It was spacious and beautifully decorated. It smelled "new". My window overlooked the garden area where the pool was located. I thought perhaps I would have a roommate, but apparently there were enough rooms for all of us. So far, this was not the military life I had expected. I could even order room service! What a pleasant outcome.

CHAPTER FOUR

Bootcamp for medical officers was not the same vigorous physical training the enlistees or draftees had to endure. Yes, we were up before dawn for rollcall, but by late afternoon our time was free. Most days were filled with classroom lectures and exams.

Each morning we had to line up in the quadrangle (which I learned was the name of a four-sided enclosure surrounded by buildings) at Fort Sam Houston[14] for rollcall. A higher-ranking officer called out our names as we stood in formation and then we replied "here". This was to determine that all of us were present according to the muster roll, which was the list of members of a military unit that also included their rank and the dates they joined or left.[15]

I remember one rainy morning I had forgotten my hat. Plus, I was late for some reason getting myself into position for rollcall after a quick egg and toast breakfast in the mess hall. Our disgusted platoon leader released me and sent me off to see the General! This should have scared me out of my wits probably, but as I calmly entered his office, I saluted him as I had learned to do from my class instruction rules, while he then proceeded to reprimand me for my incomplete apparel and tardiness. I apologized and said it would never happen again. I probably should have taken this situation more seriously, but I later found out that medical personnel did not have to follow these strict rules as did enlistees or draftees.

---

14 John Manguso, "Fort Sam Houston," *Texas State Historical Association Handbook of Texas*, TSHA Texas State Historical Association.
15 Wikipedia, "Muster (military) https://en.wikipedia.org/wiki/Muster_(military)#:~:text=A muster roll is the list of members, with roll calls) also take place in prisons.

I had problems with marching when different commands were yelled out to us. The officer in charge was not too pleased with me once again. Unfortunately, it is not easy to train a person with dyslexia how to march! For anyone not familiar with this term, it means difficulty with reading, writing, and spelling and, in my case, marching because I did not know right from left!

I was not aware I had a learning disability until I took anatomy classes. It concerned me that I had difficulty differentiating the right and left atrium of the heart as one example. I thought what is wrong with me! I received an 'A' in the course, but I had to really concentrate when taking the exam. When I was young, my teachers were perplexed when I practiced my writing skills. I would exchange one letter of the alphabet for another while never noticing the error. Years later I found out that several of us on my dad's side of the family had this affliction. My brothers and sister did not suffer from this, but several cousins did. Once we became aware of this problem mainly with spelling, we adjusted as well as we could. I failed my driving test when I was sixteen twice because when the instructor said to turn right, I turned left. So, commands given with marching were distressing for me.

I believe we picked up our uniforms at the laundry. I wondered how they knew our sizes as I was signing a release form before they were handed over to me. The Army green duffle bag was quite heavy to carry. It contained our dress blues, dress greens, and our army green fatigues. We were issued black combat boots, thick green wool socks, and the women were given a pair of dress patent leather low heels to be worn with our dress greens and more formal dress blues. When we traveled, we were instructed to wear the dress greens especially with air travel while the dress blues were for special military events.

I remember one day I had flown back home and while walking down a ramp heading toward the terminal exit, a man passing by, stopped, and said, "Wow, if I had known Army WACs looked like you, I would have joined up!" I just smiled.

I did not take the time to correct him, but I was not a WAC (Women's Army Corps) but rather a military nurse. WACs were women stationed in the Army assigned to other military duties. This women's branch of the Army was disbanded in 1978 when all units were integrated with male units.[16]

I was flattered by his comment. I tried to wear the uniform well and I felt proud to be serving my country in this way. I had not regretted my decision. I certainly felt fortunate to be a nurse in the military and not a soldier. I felt sad for what they had to endure in basic training and especially in the field of combat if they were stationed in Vietnam.

Even as a nurse, I had to learn to read maps and use coordinates. I will never forget one early afternoon after we had been transported by bus to a location in the woods somewhere outside San Antonio. Our instructor divided all of us up into squads and after giving each of us a map, a compass, and I believe binoculars, as well as carrying our backpacks filled with water and snacks, we were told to follow the coordinates listed on the map and find our way from point A to point B. My squad[17] consisted of only four nurses. Sadly, we failed the task. We read the coordinates incorrectly and by dusk we realized we were lost. Embarrassing for us, the General was notified and had to find us by helicopter before nightfall. I recall the classroom instruction seemed straight forward but using what we had learned was much more difficult in the field.

Another situation I hate to remember was going into a cave like structure where we were given gas masks and instructions on how to apply them. What now we wondered! We were told to line up against the dirt wall and when our name was called, to slowly come forward, take off our masks and shout out our serial number to the officer in charge while Tear gas was being

---

16 Wikipedia, "Women's Army Corps," https://en.wikipedia.org/wiki/Women's_Army_Corps
17 Christina Knight, "U.S. Army Units Explained: From Squads to Brigades to Corps," https://www/thirteen.org/blog-post/u-s-army-units-explaianed-from-squads-to-brigades-to-corps 2

released into the cave. The smoke-filled room gave us pause, and we understood the reason for the gas masks. After the exposure, we ran out of the cave and up a hill into the wind to relieve the burning we felt in our eyes and lungs. My lungs hurt for days after that exercise. I looked forward to the end of basic training.

Our first or second day at Fort Sam Houston was literally a painful remembrance. We had to line up in the medical building for inoculations that were given to us by a "jet injector" or pressurized jet stream that delivered percutaneous (under the skin) vaccines. I think I received six or maybe eight from this "gun". I remember my arm was sore and swollen for several days. I do not recall what vaccines were given to me at that time, but I later learned some Vietnam recruits were exposed to experimental vaccinations.[18]

I knew the seriousness of this war with one more outdoor practice that we had before this six-week course was completed. Again, wearing our combat fatigues, as we did all the days of our training, we were taken to a ground area where there were wire fences and lots of bushes along the sides and grass and dirt mounds covering the inside area (probably the size of a basketball court). We were told to crawl to the far side of this simulated war zone. What we did not know was that imitation weapons fire was directed at us the entire time coming from those bushes along the fence line on either side of us. It was a terribly frightening experience! I believe true combat soldiers had to also carry their rifles while crawling over and around these dirt mounds.

Finally, it would be remiss of me if I didn't discuss "dog tags." All recruits were issued a pair of these during basic training. We were told to put the chain, holding the tags, around our neck and never take it off under any circumstances! We showered wearing these tags! Obviously they were used for identification. The main purpose being to identify soldiers that were wounded or killed

---

18 "Vietnam Era Recruits Exposed to Experimental Vaccinations," *Jet Injectors = Jet Infectors*, https://jetinfectors.com/2017/09/29/vietnam-era-recruits-exposed-to-experimental-vaccinations/

while in the line of duty. Actually, one tag was to be worn around the neck and the other was to be placed inside a shoe. These tags were made of stainless steel and embossed with information including the soldier's first and last name, their military ID number, their blood type, and usually their religious preference. Having these tags issued to us was quite dispiriting!

Knowing that young men were forced into the Army by the draft, was really disconcerting to me. Most were barely out of high school and just eighteen years old. I was twenty-one and not mentally prepared for this no matter how much training I received. Bootcamp had to be grueling for them! They had to become "soldiers" before they could even become "men"! Why did we have to be involved in this war I asked myself? Sadly, many years later I believe, after a bit of research, I learned the answer. The wealthy and powerful of our world benefit from war, while the rest of us are used as pawns! Unconscionable!

"My goodness, what you have just explained to me about your experience as an Army nurse is so interesting. I have never read or even heard about that war! I think my grandfather might have been a soldier back then. Sadly, he passed away a few years ago. I wish I had talked to him about his experience as you talked to your grandfather about coming across this country in a covered wagon," Cyndi stated with some remorse.

"Yes, we shouldn't forget our past, especially wars. We need to understand why they occurred and how lives were tragically destroyed because of them! I know you have other patients to tend to, so I will tell you more tomorrow if you like?" I answered.

Smiling, Cyndi said, *"Yes please! I look forward to hearing more. Thanks."*

CHAPTER FIVE

Thinking back, I believe my free time got me into trouble a few times as well. I almost felt like I was not in the military when I arrived back at the hotel. In my room I found some peace and solitude. Unlike many who become energized in the company of others, I regained my emotional and spiritual energy when alone. But this solace seemed short-lived as someone was always knocking at my door.

Kelly mingled with her new dietician friends, and I found several nurses to either commiserate or spend time with. Because so many of us relaxed by the pool each afternoon, strange faces soon became familiar friendly faces.

I remember the men situated themselves on the far side of the pool, by a conscious or subconscious design, I am not sure. But undoubtedly it gave them a better perspective of their prospects while gazing across the pool. I recall a very tanned young man with black curly hair, medium build and from my view quite good-looking who kept glancing my way.

One particular afternoon, I was lying on a lounge chair taking in the warmth of the sun's rays while trying to mentally review the class instructions from earlier that day. Then one of my nursing friends startled me out of a semi-sleep.

"Susan, there is a cute guy over there staring at you. He has been watching you for a few days now. Have you noticed?"

"Yes, I have. Do you think I should be worried?" I slightly grinned as I closed my eyes, not waiting for a reply.

"Too late now, girly," was her quick response.

I heard a soft tenor voice addressing me as I slowly opened my eyes to see a man's silhouette partially blocking the bright blazing sun.

"Hello, my name is Brad. Forgive me, but I have to ask. Are you an Olympic swimmer?"

Shockingly I said, "Wow! Whatever gave you that notion?"

"Well, for one thing you have such a beautiful tan and for another you have that short hair style that so many professional swimmers seem to have," he explained.

As I laughed, I replied, "I am actually quite afraid of water, and I cannot step beyond the three-foot depth marker without becoming very short of breath or having a feeling of panic."

"I sure missed the mark on that presumption," he smiled.

Continuing, he told me, "I may be able to help you overcome that fear. Did you ever feel you were going to drown at some time in your past?"

"Yes, unfortunately my childhood best friend pushed me into the pool when I was not expecting it. I inhaled a lot of water into my lungs, and I immediately thought I was going to die," I explained as I reflected on that unusual day when I was ten years old.

Our conversation continued for several more minutes. He said he was drafted as a dentist, and it angered him that his career was disrupted. He added he couldn't wait to get back into civilian life.

He was the first of several men I became friends with who sadly were not who they presented themselves to be. I think this was one reason my parents objected so strongly to my enlistment into military service. It became quite a learning experience for me in so many ways.

I remember one hot sunny weekend afternoon Brad, as promised, decided to teach me how to swim. He told me he had been a lifeguard as well as a swimming coach. After a few simple exercises to get me used to being in the water, he surprisingly told me to step off into the 8 ft. end of the pool, drift down to the bottom, open my eyes, and then propel myself back up to the surface.

"Trust me, you can do this. I will be here for you," he said offering encouragement.

I was able to do it with only one attempt. I was impressed with his teaching skills, but soon after that I became disillusioned with his persona.

I do not remember how we arrived at his hotel room, but after luring me into bed, passion prevailed and soon he was making love to me. I felt contentment. Thoughts of my family and this ugly war were suppressed! I was enjoying the moment! We smiled at we looked into each other's eyes and embraced each other tightly with each kiss. But, later after a brief period of pleasant conversation, I suddenly noticed a light band around his left ring finger where the skin had not been exposed to the sun. I immediately knew why, of course, but I wanted to hear what he had to say.

"Brad, explain this to me," as I lifted his left hand toward his face.

He immediately began fidgeting about as he slowly offered, "Shit! Yes, Susan I'm married! My wife and I were married before I entered dental school. I might as well add, she is also eight months pregnant."

"For goodness sakes! Why in the world…?" I sadly asked.

"I am really sorry, Susan, but I felt an instant attraction to you. You are beautiful to look at, and I just wanted to spend as much time as I could with you. Obviously, you have aroused my sexual needs. Being away from home gave me a false sense of liberty. But sadly, I have taken advantage of this so-called freedom at your expense," he conveyed while trying to put his arms around me.

Pushing him away, I voiced my dissatisfaction with his attention and desires. "Call your wife when I leave and tell her how much you love her!"

I felt sick and ashamed after this encounter. But fearfully, I knew there might be more before this two-year commitment was finished if I didn't keep my guard up. I wondered if my hotel room number was being circulated among the physicians and dentists, because suddenly I was being barraged with tapping at my door by both doctors and dentists asking for a date. I always declined the invitation hoping this peculiar interest in me would subside. Why I did not with Brad I don't know. Maybe I had too much wine to drink that afternoon. I still felt a connection to Jeff, especially since he was planning to come down to San Antonio in a few more weeks to spend time with me before he began his six-week training.

During this war, physicians had a military obligation. It was called the Berry Plan enacted in 1954.[19] They were offered three choices regarding their commitment. Jeff decided to choose the first option of going into active duty after finishing his internship. The plan ended in 1973.

I was introduced to him by another boyfriend, Tom, whom I had met when I first started working at a local hospital after graduation. He was an extern, meaning he had completed two of his four years of medical school. I loved his dedication and compassion to the patients he was assigned to as well as the long hours he spent in the lab doing research with a well renowned physician. Unfortunately, my attraction towards him was not met with the same measure of attraction towards me. I liked spending time with him, and he taught me so much regarding medical practice that I could also apply to the care of my patients as a nurse. But as I said before, I was not interested in getting married and definitely not to a physician.

I had made up my mind after high school graduation, that if I did decide to marry, I wanted that man to be an artist. Being an artist myself, I felt we had a vision and clarity of the world that

---

19 Wikipedia, "Berry Plan," *Military, Conscription in the United States, United States in the Vietnam War*, https://military.wikia.org/wiki/Berry_Plan

others did not possess. Call me haughty, if you will, but I did not feel most physicians had that vision and clarity. Their focus was on science. Plus, during my first year as a new graduate nurse, I witnessed and heard of too many "Peyton Place" activities going on in remote areas of the hospital. I didn't want that in my life.

Peyton Place was a 1956 novel by Grace Metalious which was released also as a film a year later. A soup opera on an American TV network from the years 1964 – 1969 was also created based on this novel. The story revolved around a small town in New England after WW II where scandal and moral hypocrisy contradicted the tranquil illusion thought to be exhibited in the community.[20]

As I said, this Peyton Place was evident to my eyes by the many liaisons of medical personnel. I did not want to have to worry about my physician husband coming home late at night. Not because he was saving a patient's life, but because he was having an affair with another hospital employee.

Unaware of my personal convictions, Tom believed our feelings for each other were reciprocal. So, his plan was to take me to Las Vegas for a quick little wedding chapel ceremony, unbeknownst to me, while on a sightseeing trip driving through the southern U.S.

Seeing the Grand Canyon, Bryce Canyon, Zion National Park, and Hoover Dam were wonders I thought I might never get to see. So thanks to Tom, I was really enjoying myself until we arrived in Las Vegas late one night. I recall our sleeping quarters were in someone's attractively decorated basement. Possibly it was the home of one of his friends. I woke up after a restless night on a sleeper sofa in the middle of the recreation room. As I looked up, I saw him coming down the stairs.

---

20 Wikipedia, "Peyton Place (novel)," https://en.wikipedia.org/w/index.php?title=Peyton_Place_(novel)&oldid=1102275299" last edited (2022)

He smiled as he approached and after falling on top of me, he explained, "It is time to get up. We are going to a chapel in about two hours. So, get ready."

"What do you mean we are going to a chapel?" I questioned.

"We will be married in just a few hours from now," he replied nonchalantly.

"What! Why didn't you tell me you had this plan?" I asked looking at his face three inches away as he tried giving me a good morning kiss.

Staring up at him, I immediately returned with, "I am just starting my nursing career, and you have to finish medical school and then a residency. What if I become pregnant? We are not ready for this responsibility! Absolutely not! We are too young! I am only twenty and you are twenty-three. Gracious!"

He looked at me with surprise and disgust and stated, "Why do you think I took you home to meet my parents, my brother, and his wife as well as our neighbors and other family friends? It wasn't just a pleasure trip. Dam it!"

"Well, I am sorry. I wish you had consulted me first on what should have been a mutual decision," I replied while turning away to get out of bed.

The drive back to Denver was extremely uncomfortable for both of us. He was furious, especially since he told all the hospital interns that we would be married by the time we returned. He often told me they wanted me, and he had me. His pride was irrevocably damaged!

With that long silence, my mind took me to another unsettling remembrance. Tom asked me to fly back to Baltimore for the weekend just prior to senior graduation. Many classmates were having a party, and he wanted to "show me off" to his friends. He requested I prepare a meal for one of his best friends and his wife the Friday night before the upcoming party. I loved to cook, so I agreed. I decided to make duck ala orange. Tom bought several bottles of expensive wine that he could easily afford for the occasion.

After a triumphant dinner, for which I owe credit to the famous chef James Beard, Tom and his friend finished their discussion about whether socialized medicine would flow into the US as it had in Canada. With their bellies full, they mutually agreed we should go "bar hopping". I looked toward Martin's wife, Brenda, and she appeared to agree with the idea. I didn't even know what this phrase meant. But off we went. Three bars later, I began to feel sick. I didn't want to throw up on the sidewalk, so I asked Tom to take me back to his apartment as quickly as possible. I remember I could barely walk, and after telling them I needed to be excused, I decided to go to bed. I could hear laughter and talking in the living room, but I could not make out what was being discussed.

Within minutes after changing into my nightgown, Tom tiptoes into the room and laying on top of me on the bed, gives me a kiss. Looking into my eyes, which many times he stated were beautiful, he whispers, "Honey, Martin wants to swap".

"What do you mean Martin wants to swap?" I asked while hoping this severe headache would soon go away.

"You know. He wants to have sex with you while I have sex with his wife."

Starring at him, trying to understand why, I instantly thought about Martin's wife and how she might feel about this. I remember her as being very pretty when Tom introduced her when they arrived. She had long black hair, dark brown eyes, and appeared quite dainty or even fragile. She seemed a little shy as well. Whereas Martin, to be polite, was stocky and had an expanded waistline. I decided this was due to too much drinking and probably not getting enough exercise with the tremendous amount of required studying. Also a bald spot around the top of his head was hard not to miss. He was too boisterous for my taste, and he demonstrated a certain confidence that disturbed me. I thought to myself that someday his ego just might get him into trouble. I was acutely aware of how intelligent both he and Tom were, based on the topics they discussed during dinner. Otherwise, he was not appealing to me in the least, and I thought perhaps his marriage to Brenda had been arranged with the help of their parents. They did not seem to be a good match. I felt the marriage would not last long unless she just wanted to be known as the wife of a physician.

I had never heard of the words "wife swapping" until that night, and I hoped I would never hear this phrase again. Tom tried to explain this was the norm now among young couples. Really?

"Definitely not! I will not be party to this! For goodness' sake, I cannot imagine doing such a thing. Tell them I have a severe headache (which is true), and please ask them to go home!"

After the senior medical school party that next night, I was happy to fly back home.

We did remain friends I guess, since we kindly greeted each other as we passed in the hospital corridors. He occasionally asked me to join him for lunch in the cafeteria when he had the time. I knew he was hoping I would reconsider and change my mind about marrying him, but this was not a consideration for me, especially then.

During one lunch "date", Tom and I were sitting at a cafeteria table when Jeff approached. He was about 5'10" with long curly blond hair. He wore a tie-dyed bandana around his head and a small chain of beads was attached to the bell of the stethoscope hanging around his neck. On his right wrist was a wide black leather watchband. He only looked the part of a doctor because he was wearing his short white lab coat over green scrubs. I wondered to myself how he could get away with this somewhat unprofessional attire. But the hippie culture was encroaching, especially in Colorado in the late 60's. So, I guess some leniency was allowed. After a brief introduction, Tom told me Jeff graduated from the same medical school and came to Colorado to do some skiing during his internship. They talked a bit about professors and classes while I sat quietly eating my chicken salad sandwich and sipping my Dr. Pepper. When it was time for Tom to visit one of his patients, he put his hand on Jeff's shoulder and asked him to take care of me. I wasn't sure what that meant, but by this time Tom probably realized it was fruitless to ask me again to marry him. I assumed he wanted someone to spy on my activities after he left to feel some sense of retribution.

I am not sure how well that plan worked as Jeff, and I became good friends. We spent a lot of time together at the city park playing frisbee or taking rides through the mountains on his new motorcycle. He introduced me to a few authors whose writings he appreciated, among them were Herman Hesse and Kurt Vonnegut. After reading four of Herman Hesse's books: *Demian*, *Steppenwolf*, *Siddhartha*, and *The Glass Bead Game*, I became spellbound as well.

Herman Hesse was a German-Swiss poet, novelist, and painter. His writings explored an individual's search for self-knowledge, authenticity, and spirituality. Post WWI youth found his writings to be enlightening. This popularity also continued during the time of the Vietnam war.[21]

The author, Kurt Vonnegut, had a life filled with pessimism after his wealthy parents suffered great monetary loss due to the Depression. The Wall Street Crash of 1929 disrupted so many lives, especially the rich who invested in the stock market. Many committed suicide.

Vonnegut entered WWII at the age of 20 and was captured by the Germans in the Battle of the Bulge. As a POW (prisoner of war) he was sent to Dresden. British and American bombers destroyed the city with a firestorm, killing up to 60,000 civilians. POWs survived because they were housed in an old meat locker 60 feet below ground.

---

21   Wikipedia, "Herman Hesse," https://en.wikipedia.org>wiki>Herman_Hesse.

In the early 1970's Vonnegut was one of the most famous writers in the world. He was referred to as having the black comic voice. He could make his audiences laugh; despite the horrors he described in his books. He believed in preserving our Constitutional freedoms. But he believed that corporate greed, overpopulation, and war would win out in the end. His quote, "We could have saved the world, but we were just too damned lazy" was stated often. *Slaughterhouse Five*, considered one of the world's great antiwar books, was read by many young men who faced the draft during the Vietnam War.[22]

Jeff and I soon became known throughout the hospital as the "hippy couple". I knew why Jeff fit that mold, but I was not sure about myself. I remember one night when he was on call, he had to go to the ER (emergency room) to see a patient, and sadly he arrived barefoot after racing down a back stairway from his call room! Obviously, he was summoned to the administrator's office for a reprimand that next morning. I wondered if I really wanted to be associated with him.

Unfortunately, during those early 70's, drugs were widely experimented with, LSD being one of them. I don't know if Jeff may have tried that, but quite common was the use of hashish and weed or marijuana, both of which come from the cannabis plant. Jeff told me he preferred hashish, and I recall he kept it in a cereal box hidden in the cupboard among the other cereal boxes. He also relayed to me that most of the interns were "high" when they went on morning rounds. I was displeased to hear that, but unfortunately this was that era.

Timothy Leary, a psychologist, and author of books advocating the use of LSD, became a cult leader during the 1960's. He received his doctorate in psychology from the University of California at Berkeley in 1950. He became a lecturer at Harvard University in 1959. With his experimentation of certain mushrooms, he concluded that psychedelic drugs could

---

22 William Rodney Allen, "A Brief Biography of Kurt Vonnegut," *Kurt Vonnegut Museum * Library*

be effective in transforming personality and expanding human consciousness. But by 1963 he was dismissed from Harvard because his experiments were too highly controversial. He was arrested in 1965 and 1968 for possession of marijuana.[23]

Soldiers in Vietnam began using drugs while off duty just to cope with this war. By 1971, 51% smoked marijuana, 28% had used heroin or cocaine, and 31% had used psychedelics such as LSD or mushrooms. Sadly, many were still addicted when they returned home. The military discharged between 1,000 and 2,000 heroin addicts per month.[24]

In 1968 Richard Nixon was elected to the presidency, running on a platform of "law and order" as a response to the rising use of cannabis and heroin by Americans not only in the military, but also the counterculture hippies of the Woodstock generation. He established the Controlled Substances Act (CSA) in 1970. This statute established regulation of possession, use, distribution, importation, and manufacturing of certain substances. Since 1970 this act has been amended numerous times.[25]

I smoked weed during that era, maybe twice and did not like the effect it had on me. I was not that true "free spirit" after all. But Jeff did not seem to object. He said he enjoyed being with me anyway.

I remember during one of our early dates, he said he really appreciated that I did not "talk shop" like other nurses he had dated. He was excited one evening when I told him I could not go out with him because I had to be at the Tri-state Auto Show that evening.

"What! Why?" he asked.

---

[23] Britiannica, The Editors of Encyclopaedia. "Timothy Leary" Encyclopedia Britannica, 27 May 2022 https://www.britannica.com/Timothy-Leary. Accessed 12 August 2022

[24] "Drugs in the Vietnam War," A Story Map (https://storymaps.arcgis.com) (https://www.esri.com) 2

[25] Danielle Corcione, "How Nixon Established The War On Drugs As We Know It," *Navigation* Published: November 26, 2018

"Because I am one of the "models" selected to escort guys onto the stage to receive trophies for their auto and motorcycle exhibits," I explained without any hesitation.

"Wow! How did this come about; you working as a model, I mean?" he continued to ask.

"Well, I needed money for tuition and when a modeling agency came to the house to sign my sister to do TV commercials, I decided I wanted to try modeling, too. Fortunately, they accepted me as well. I was tall enough at 5'7 ½ inches and my weight was in the range they preferred for models at 115 pounds. I took night classes for TV, ramp modeling and photography. Also, I had the voice for TV, I guess. I didn't do any TV commercials, like my sister did, but I did advertising events for companies such as this event tonight. It is fun and I get to meet interesting people who are not in the medical field, which I also like."

"I love you! Do you mind if I come to see you do your "thing" tonight?" he asked.

"Sure, that should be okay. You might enjoy looking at all the shiny chrome souped up cars and motorcycles! Those of us from the modeling agency have to arrive an hour early for photos, but you can come any time after that."

Suddenly, I recalled Dr. Macrae assigning Jeff to mom's case during her hospital stay. I wondered if it was because he knew Jeff and I were dating each other.

I had never planned on entering the military, even though the war news upset me, and I wanted to help in some way. But, after my mother's surgeon stopped me in the hallway to say he needed to speak to me, my new career path was forged.

Leading me into the supply room of the surgical ward where I was working at the time, Dr. Macrae explained, "Susan, I have done everything I can for your mother, but I couldn't get all the cancer even with the surgery. Sadly, she will not survive this. I do not want your father or mother or even the rest of the family to know this sad outcome. Your mother will not be able to accept the news. The surgical procedure I performed will be disconcerting to her. With your medical knowledge, I know you can be discreet with this information."

I could not believe what I was hearing from him. My mother was so faithful about having her yearly medical exams and check-ups for cancer detection. There was no history of cancer in the family as I recalled. She was only forty-eight years old, too young for this grim outcome! Now knowing her fate, I cried and cried. Fortunately, no one walking past the supply room could hear me, I thought. The surgeon left after giving me a hug and soon the Head Nurse as well as the Nursing Director came into the room, and after some comforting words, they told me to go home for the rest of the day.

I had to compose myself for the drive home, so I decided to page Jeff. Thankfully, he said he would be free in a half hour. Being mom's intern, I was certain he knew what I had just been told.

"Meet me at our favorite spot across the street in the park. I will be there in about twenty minutes," he stated before quickly hanging up the receiver.

Those minutes really seemed like hours to me, but when he arrived, I felt such relief. He would appreciate what I was dealing with and give me reassuring words. A picnic table was nearby and after running toward me and giving me a strong hug and kiss, he jumped up on the top of the table and paced back and forth, thinking about how I should handle this problem. After a few minutes, he jumped down and said I should consider joining the Army. I would be away from home and not have to worry about exposing mom's fate to the rest of the family. He said I could get leave time when it was necessary to return without any difficulty. We can be together for basic training and, hopefully, get the same duty station.

I do not remember how long it took me to make that decision, but I found myself at the recruiting office and signing up for the

Army Nurse Corps. Unfortunately, I didn't ask Jeff when his entry date was, and I signed to go to San Antonio six weeks before he did. We were both upset at my hastiness, but he said he would come down two weeks early so we could be together for at least that short time. I felt some guilt at abandoning mom and the rest of the family, but I believed this was the best decision under the circumstances.

CHAPTER SIX

I heard from Jeff a few times with letters and an occasional phone call. And as promised, I did receive that call a few days before my fifth week of training.

"Hi Susan, I am making plans to fly down next Monday," he said excitedly.

After some silence, I hesitantly replied, "Oh Jeff, I am so sorry but please don't come. I know what I am about to say will shock you; I'm engaged."

"Susan, did you just say what I thought you said?"

"I know it is terribly sudden, and I don't want to explain how this happened," I paused, while waiting for his next response.

"I can't believe it! You are blowing my mind right now! We just talked two weeks ago, and everything was fine between us. I told my parents about you and how I felt our relationship was moving forward. My God! Are you losing it?" he yelled.

"Is he a physician? Are you pregnant?"

"The answer to your first question is possibly, but doubtful; to the second no, and to the third no," I emphatically responded.

Not waiting for his response, I continued, "I will admit that being away from home for this length of time may have affected my judgement. Plus, I was pressured into making this decision. I can't go into it now, and I hope someday you will be able to forgive me. My explanation might offer you some solace. I really need to say goodbye," not wanting to prolong this grief for him any longer.

I should not have ended our conversation so abruptly, but my finance, Charlie, knowing Jeff was going to call, was knocking at my hotel room door. I decided I needed to quickly end the call to avoid any confrontation that might develop between them. I never heard from Jeff again.

"How did he take the news?" Charlie asked almost triumphantly.

"As you would expect naturally," I explained with some discomfort.

"Listen, if you don't mind, I would like to be alone for a while. I've hurt him, and I feel sad about that, so please forgive me. I will call you later," as I ushered him toward the door.

My mind led me back to my decision to never marry. I did not want to complicate my life or someone else's with this lifelong commitment. I never wanted to have children and that alone was not fair to a perspective partner. I thought we lived in a cruel world and bringing up children in this ugly world was almost unconscionable. Also, the lack of nurturing from my mother during my childhood, did not give me the skills I thought necessary for child rearing with the ample love and devotion that a child needed. I do not believe my thought process was ever conveyed to Jeff, and if it had, I am sure my engagement baffled him even more.

As I mentioned earlier, I grew up thinking I was ugly. I sensed this from my mother, and I saw it in the mirror. My sister was the pretty daughter in our family, and she received a lot of attention from family, friends, and relatives because of her striking beauty. I was shoved into the background at family gatherings. I grew to accept this, and since I was quite shy anyway, it seemed the norm for me. Consequently, I was not invited to parties like the popular kids in school. I also lacked that socialization that developed during those early teenage years. I was the "wallflower." My high school had several clicks of which I belonged to none. I had maybe one or two friends. It was an incredibly sad and somewhat scary time for me while I was going through my adolescence years. My first real date happened when I was a senior. He was a football star, and something or someone made him ask me out. Maybe it was a bet with his friends. I had my first kiss on that date. I felt terribly awkward and nervous, which I believe he sensed, so I never heard from him after that Saturday night. But during my senior year, a physical transformation was beginning. A swan was being created!

Officers and enlistees were not to fraternize, especially at the clubs located on the Army post. Therefore, the clubs were segregated. After a full day of classes and some marching, many new recruits would gather at these clubs at night for relaxation and to garnish that feeling of camaraderie or togetherness. There was lots of laughter, beer drinking, pool playing and, of course, dancing.

Because of my lack of social skills, I never really learned to dance well. But, to my surprise, when I did follow my friends into the officers' club, I was almost immediately approached by guys asking me to step onto the floor for that "light fandango". Obviously, I was not used to all this attention. It even worried me a little. I sometimes wondered if I was a witch! Probably half the time I accepted their request, but I usually prefaced with, "I really don't know how to dance." Their reply was, "Don't worry. It is easy, and I will make sure we don't step on each other's toes!" We would laugh and the tension soon melted away.

About twice a week one of my new nursing friends, Mary, and I would go to the club, only because she wanted someone to go with her. She loved to flirt, I guess. The room was filled with cigarette smoke, and the music was too loud for my taste. But gulping down a few beers seemed to rectify that problem. After about the second trip to the officer's club, we were approached by two young men who wanted to sit at our table. They were quite handsome, but after spending a few minutes talking with them, I decided they were too young and immature for my taste. Tom was three years older than me, and Jeff was four years older. I believed these guys were at least a year younger than we were.

They continued however to give reasons why they were our age, twenty-one. They said they were Warrant Officers.

In 1965 twenty-one MSC (Medical Service Corps) officers had been killed in Vietnam. As the demand for medical officers rose, it was decided to have warrant officers become aeromedical pilots or "dustoff pilots" a name that was coined in 1963 by the 57th Medical Detachment deployed out of Fort Meade, Maryland.[26] They used that term "dustoff" in their code book for Hueys taking off from the dry dusty countryside of Vietnam. That name then represented all MedEvac helicopter operations for the remainder of that war.[27]

Charlie and his friend Mike were in the ten-week training program at Fort Sam Houston to become part of the four-man crews on these Hueys.[28] Due to the size of the helicopters, they became easy targets. The crewmen were risking their lives when they flew into the heavy "hot zones" or combat areas of the jungles in Vietnam to rescue the wounded soldiers as well as Vietnamese men, women, and children. This type of rescue was necessary because of the jungle terrain and heavy combat. Roads were not useable even if nearby.

These warrant officers were usually assigned to regiments fighting in the most brutal battlefield areas, mainly in the northern region of South Vietnam referred to as I-Core.[29] They did not have bullet proof helmets or body armor as did the ground troops. However, they did carry weapons. While ground troops could get down into bunkers for protection from flying bullets, the medics had to move swiftly toward enemy fire to retrieve the wounded and evacuate the area as quickly as possible to avoid being wounded or killed themselves.

---

26   U.S. Army Medical Department Office of Medical History, "Medical Department Organization," Chapter 11, 338.
27   Jack Beckett, "'Dead Men Flying' Heroic as Hell – The Dustoff Pilots of The Vietnam War (image heavy)" War *History Online, The Place for Military History News and Views. August 21, 2015*
28   Military Machine, "The AH-1 Cobra By Bell Helicopter"
29   Vietnam Battlefield, "Corps Tactical Zones"

As Charlie and Mike explained the details of their impending one-year assignment, the stark reality of the hazards of this war came to light for me. I do not remember the statistics they gave of medical warrant officers returning home alive from this tour of duty, but I believe it was between ten and fifteen percent! So sad!

"Aren't you afraid?" I asked while taking a deep breath.

"Sure, but this is war, and this is what we signed up to do. We want to help save lives over there, especially our own soldiers. From the tests we had to take, we were told we had the aptitude for this medical training and helicopter piloting, so we accepted this assignment with honor," Charlie proudly explained.

Soon Mary and I had developed a fondness for them. We spent a lot of time together, not only at the officer's club, but also at our hotel and enjoying the city nightlife as well.

Two weeks after being introduced, Charlie asked me to marry him. I was shocked at the suddenness of his request. He informed me that his instructor thought we were well suited for each other and even the rest of his classmates wanted us to be together. His pleading went on for another week to the point it was wearing me down. So, I relented and said "yes."

I feel apologetic about revealing why I decided to accept his proposal. I do not want to think of myself as callous, but it might seem that way to others. Charlie said he absolutely loved me, and he was going to name his Huey after me and paint my name on the side of the helicopter.

He wanted to take a portfolio containing photographs of me from my modeling days with him when he left for Vietnam. I was reluctant initially, but I acquiesced and let him have the pictures.

For some unknown reason to me, I had packed this portfolio into my suitcase for the trip to San Antonio. Maybe I wanted to remember my past life before entering military servitude. I don't really know but thinking back on it I feel embarrassed to have brought those pictures along.

I honestly felt that because of his treacherous job, he would become one of the statistics he told me about and not return alive. I feared that same fate for his best friend Mike, too. Maybe knowing he was engaged to be married to this girl, looking back at him through those photos, might give him a feeling of hopefulness at the end of a grueling day saving lives in that war laden combat zone. To my mind, I thought I was being benevolent without considering the "what ifs" should he return from his tour unscathed. I soon realized my altruistic gesture was short lived.

CHAPTER SEVEN

Before Charlie received his orders for Vietnam, my six-week bootcamp training was finished and I had to pack for my move to El Paso, Texas where I would receive my three-month operating room course that I requested at the recruiter's office. Just before I was to depart, I received his engagement ring, which was small, but what he could afford on a warrant officer's salary. When he put it on my finger, surprisingly, I suddenly felt a strong commitment to this relationship. I was going to remain faithful for that year long separation.

As luck would have it, Mary had also requested the same surgical course. So, we decided to share an apartment located just across the street from William Beaumont Hospital where our classes were located. We didn't have a car, so the location was quite welcome. If we needed to go shopping, we just took a bus downtown. We loved our fully furnished two-bedroom apartment. Soon we came to know most of the residents of this complex since many of us were part of the medical staff for this hospital at Fort Bliss.

Mary wanted to have a party shortly after we settled into our new home to get to know our neighbors better. Honestly, I knew she was looking for a prospective husband. I don't recall how many attended, but it was a success. Charlie came to visit me that same weekend; fortunately, he was quite helpful with the food preparation for the party.

I remember four guys who shared the same apartment in the next building arriving separately, which I found a little odd. Mary really wanted one of them to come because she noticed him tanning near the pool shortly after we moved in. He was tall, slender, with very blond almost white hair and blue eyes. She told me once or twice she was only interested in men with blond hair and blue eyes. So, in her mind this was the man for her.

There were only a few other girls at our party, and they were either nurses or dieticians. The ratio of women to men was about one to four. But no one seemed to mind. I also noticed that Mary and I as well as the other girls outranked the guys. We were officers while they were enlistees and had ranks from private to sergeant and, of course, warrant officer which was Charlie's rank.

During basic training it was stressed time and again that officers were not to fraternize with the enlistees. That was one reason for the two nightclubs on post, one for enlistees and the other for officers. As I mentioned before, we abided by these rules until we arrived back at our hotel in the late afternoon while going through basic training. We welcomed the friendship of Charlie and Mike even though we outranked them. I honestly think they were proud to be dating officers of higher rank.

Something else I noticed differently among the officers and the enlistees was that most of the enlistees were college graduates. Some had their master's degrees, and a few had been working on their doctorates before they received their draft notice. Sad that their education had to be interrupted for this war, I thought. Many were much more intelligent than their commanding officers, and consequently, it was difficult for them to take orders. This created problems for the military during that war.

While Charlie was helping me mix up some dip for the chips, there was a loud knock at the kitchen door, the easiest entrance because it was on the pool side of the building. I rushed to open the door, and when I looked into the eyes of this stranger, I felt an instant attraction that I couldn't quite explain. He was the last to arrive of those four roommates who lived in the adjacent complex. Being the best hostess I could be, I introduced him to those he had not already met, including Mary and Charlie.

I was able to spend a short amount of time talking with him. He said he didn't really like parties but wanted to see who lived in this apartment. I thought to myself, I wouldn't want to get on his bad side simply because of his muscular build. He was not tall, maybe 5'11", but he looked like he certainly could have won a body building contest from what I could tell!

I remember seeing him from time to time soon after we arrived in El Paso. Sometimes when I gazed out the kitchen window while washing dishes, I would see him pass by heading to the laundry room. He had his military whites piled up into a heap under his arm while his long curly brown hair fell over his right eye. I wasn't sure how he got away with this longer hair length. All draftees had their heads shaved the first day of their arrival at bootcamp, and it was to remain trimmed throughout their enlistment. He was always wearing shorts and sandals when he was at the pool, and his strong physique was evident with those bulging calf muscles.

He only stayed a short time at our soiree. I offered him wine and beer, but he told me he didn't drink alcohol. He only drank water or sodas, preferably cola. So, after he had a can of Coca-Cola and a few chips, he was on his way.

Charlie didn't appear to mind that I spent a few minutes talking with this stranger as he loved being surrounded by people just having a good time. Mary soon nestled into a corner of the living room sitting on the lap of her new friend Jack. So, I played hostess and made sure everyone had plenty of food and drinks to keep them happy.

As the evening wore on and the last of the crowd had finally left, Mary and Charlie helped with the cleanup.

"How was your new date, Mary?" I winked as I finished washing the last of the dishes.

Blushing slightly, she replied gleefully, "Oh Susan, I think I found my true love!"

"Oh really? So quickly. How can you be so sure?" I asked.

"Remember, I told you I wanted a husband with blue eyes and blond hair."

"Yes, I remember you mentioned that." I was also thinking of the many conversations Mary, and I had about our lives prior to entering the military.

It seemed important to her to have her children look "Caucasian," a term no longer used for skin color and native origin. I wondered if she had been taunted by children at school when she was young. I certainly didn't see any reason for that to occur, but children could be quite cruel. She had beautifully tanned, olive colored skin and dark brown eyes with lustrous dark brown hair. She was quite cute and had a fun-loving nature. She said she inherited her mother's features, as she was small in stature and very thin. She ate constantly but couldn't add those extra pounds, and complained of having to wear a child's bra, even after entering her twenties.

We became good friends during basic training, and she endorsed my engagement to Charlie. We had lots of discussions well into the night about what we hoped life would be like after we left the service. She often expressed her desire to have lots of children, and she repeatedly mentioned they would all have blond hair and blue eyes. So, for whatever reason, it was a high priority for her, as well as having a highly educated husband.

Charlie had a few more weeks remaining before his one-year Vietnam commitment began. He decided I needed to meet his family, so after requesting my only week of vacation from my OR course, we took that trip. I was nervous to meet them, of course. Since he was a Catholic, I was not surprised when he told me he was one of twelve children. Wow!

I remember when I called my parents to let them know I was engaged, they were once again upset with me. My father answered the phone and with a brief congratulatory remark he handed the phone to my mother. He had always been a man of few words and rarely expressed his views or passed judgment, unless it was monumental.

As weak as she probably was from her illness, she remarked, "What in the world! How long have you known him? It cannot be long enough for you to make this kind of commitment! What is his religion?"

"He is Catholic mom," I said knowing her voice would reverberate throughout the room.

"Catholic! You can't marry a Catholic! We refuse to accept this!" she yelled.

Sadly, as a Lutheran I was raised to avoid those in the Catholic religion. There was a Catholic church across the street from our church, and it was as if there was a barbed wire fence separating the two. That imaginary line was never to be crossed. We could be friends with them at school and partake of their Friday night fish dinners. But marry, never! That was forbidden! I remember one of my cousins married a Catholic, and her mother (my dad's sister) never spoke to her for years after that. Astonishing!

The history behind this severe division stemmed from the excommunication of Martin Luther from the Catholic church. He had been ordained into the priesthood in 1507. Soon he rejected several teachings and practices of the Roman Catholic Church. He believed salvation and eternal life was not earned by good deeds. Prior to his death, he even expressed antagonism for Jews and called for the burning of their synagogues and their deaths. This rhetoric was not just directed at the Jews, but also Roman Catholics, Anabaptists, and nontrinitarian Christians. He died in 1546 with Pope Leo X's excommunication still in effect.[30]

"Mom, I don't think God cares what religious beliefs we espouse or embrace. We are on this earth to love one another period," I tried to explain.

---

30   Wikipedia, "Martin Luther," https://en.Wikipedia.org>wiki>Martin_Luther

I don't remember how our conversation ended, but I know it wasn't pleasant, as happened with most of our conversations during my youth.

Charlie and I loaded up his beloved powerful car, a 1968 400/442 Oldsmobile Cutlass and drove west through the desert terrain on our way to California.

While I was looking ahead at the "pool of water" mirages in the highway and the many green cacti sparsely scattered across the desert countryside, I was startled when he suddenly stopped by the side of the road.

"Susan, I have something to tell you before we go any further," he stated as he stretched his right arm over the top of the seat toward me.

Oh my. Suddenly my experience with Brad came to mind! My imagination sometimes drifted toward the dark side, as I was accused of many times in my youth.

"Okay, I am ready for the worst," I said, looking at his expression for some hint of what he might disclose.

Hesitantly he continued, "I lied about my age. You were right, I am not twenty-one. I am nineteen. When I spotted you at that table in the Officers club, I knew immediately I had to get to know you. I was afraid you would reject me if I told you the truth."

I wasn't surprised at this odd confession, but I was glad it wasn't what I thought the revelation would be. Immediately, I realized he was the age of my brothers. How awful. I remember friends of my brothers would come over to our house, and I sensed their interest in me. I couldn't stand it. Gracious! But now here I was engaged to this "boy!"

I took a long pause before replying. My brain decided to think about what lies might he disclose in the future if this relationship moved forward. Almost instantly I thought about Tim. Did he explain to Kathy his interest in asking me out before they were married? That relationship disturbed me, and I knew I wanted an honest faithful marriage, if I married at all.

"Well, obviously I am upset and somewhat angry that you lied to me. I do have this ring on my finger now, so I will remain committed to this relationship. That is all I have to say," looking away and not waiting for his comment.

After a few more hours of driving, he decided he needed to take a break and asked me to take the wheel. After reading the paper for a short time, he fell asleep. I could barely stand seeing the long stretches of highway staring back at me. I was tired of looking at miles of sandy hills and wanted to fall asleep too. Several hours later, I saw flashing red lights in the rear-view mirror. Great! I calmly pulled over to the side of the road while a policeman got out of his patrol car and walked toward the driver side of the car. As I leaned my head out the window, he stooped down with a stern glare looking directly at me.

"Do you know how fast you were going, young lady?" he gruffly inquired.

"Sorry, I really don't," I sheepishly replied, wondering if Charlie was going to come to my rescue.

"I have been following you for about sixty miles, trying to catch up to you! You have been traveling over 120 miles per hour!" he retorted as he pulls out his pen and paper to write a ticket.

At this point, Charlie awakened and leaned forward to look at the officer. He explained that he was leaving for Vietnam in a few weeks, and we were heading to California to visit his parents. This must have triggered some emotion in the cop. After giving me the ticket and explaining I had to see the judge that following Monday morning, he said he thought the judge might be lenient with me even though this was Barstow County, and judges were extremely strict with their rulings. Charlie paid my $60 fine, and he and the judge seemed to get along quite well, so I was relieved.

Mike met us when we arrived in Rosemont later that same day. He invited his new girlfriend, Karen, who happened to have been in the same OR course as Mary and me. I don't remember how or when he met her. I do recall she had been a nun before deciding to become a nurse and enter military service. I was shocked at this sudden metamorphosis. She had to be at least five years older than Mike. I guess age didn't matter to them as much as it did to me.

A few days later sitting together in the back seat of Charlie's parents' car while his father was driving us to a family wedding, his mother looked back from the passenger seat. She mentioned twice to Charlie that she had seen Vickie, his hometown girlfriend, several times after he left for bootcamp. Apparently, she had asked about him, and I sensed still cared for him. I could tell his mother really wanted that relationship to work. Bringing up her name made me feel that she was not in favor of our union at all. I think, like me, she felt I was too old for Charlie. The family relatives greeted me warmly at the wedding, but there was a lot of dancing, and I know my awkwardness didn't win them over.

We spent a lot of time with Mike and Karen which was quite fun and therapeutic for all of us. Mike had already said goodbye to his family in Tennessee since he and Charlie were going to take the same flight to Vietnam. I was happy about that. They really needed each other right now.

Just hours before Karen and I had to fly back to El Paso, I came downstairs to have some breakfast. I didn't see Charlie and was told by his mother he went out for a walk.

"He seemed to have a lot on his mind," she said while standing in front of the stove frying bacon and not looking directly at me.

I felt she was hoping he wanted to let me know the engagement was off. I decided I should go look for him. I found Charlie sitting on the dusty ground in a cornfield just a few blocks from his parents' home. I wasn't really surprised at seeing him sitting there among some corn stalks. The sun's rays were shining down on his teary-eyed face. He had been in deep thought. Not about releasing me from this commitment, but rather about his possible life or death fate. Most of these soldiers wondered if they would ever see their families again. How long was their time on this earth? What a horrible thing to have to contemplate; I could not even imagine. I sat down beside him and comforted his as best I could. A few hours later when the taxi arrived for Karen and me, we said our goodbyes, not knowing if we would ever see each other again.

CHAPTER EIGHT

While Karen and I were away that week in California, Mary's relationship with Jack intensified. But instead of feeling joyful, she seemed troubled. Finally, one afternoon she said she needed to speak to me. Since we shared our deepest thoughts and concerns, I was worried.

"Susan, you know how much I love Jack?" she asked as if waiting for a positive affirmation to calm her fretfulness.

"Yes, I guess I do, Mary. You seem to spend all your free time with him".

"Remember that weekend a few months ago when you flew back home to see your folks? Without waiting for my answer, she continued, "Well, that was the first and only time I slept with Jack. Honestly, I swear on the Bible!"

After a short pause.... "Susan, I haven't had a period since then. I am so scared! I think I am pregnant. The Army is going to kick me out; I just know it! That's in the rule book! They will be furious that I have been here less than three months, and I won't be able to pay back the four years I owe for my college education. But I really want this child!" she confided while tears were streaming down her cheeks.

"Have you told Jack?" I asked somewhat surprised that this happened on her first and only sexual encounter with him but wanting to believe her sincerity.

I gave her a hug while trying to think of reassuring words of comfort.

She quickly answered while wiping away the tears, "Not yet. I want to get tested first to make sure. I know he will marry me; I just don't want a dishonorable discharge."

"Don't worry about that. I am sure this has happened to many young women in all the military branches. The Army can adapt," hoping my answer gave her some comfort.

I don't remember the exact date that Mary left for home with her discharge papers in hand, but she and Jack were married by an Army Chaplain, which pleased both of us. Jack received a master's degree in psychology before he was drafted, and his plan was to pursue his doctorate after discharge. I felt her future was bright; her life dreams would be fulfilled. I envisioned her with lots of blue-eyed blond babies.

Soon after she left, Jack had a new duty station, which I believe was Vietnam. Sadly, I never stayed in touch with Mary or Karen after I left the military, and I regret that so much. Forty years later, I tried finding Mary and saw that the person who fit her description had had four children, but I noticed she was no longer married to Jack. I wrote her a letter at the address provided from my research, but unfortunately, I never received a reply.

Pregnancy in the U.S. military had been a "hot potato" issue since WWII, and the services never did really know how to deal with it until much later. In 1951 President Harry S. Truman signed an Executive Order giving the military branches permission to discharge a woman if she became pregnant, gave birth to a child, or became a parent by adoption or a stepparent. This was taken as an ironclad mandate, and military women who became pregnant were summarily discharged per new regulations. When women became more aware of their rights under the law, the military revisited the pregnancy issue. Alas, in 1971, just months after Mary was discharged, they instituted a policy of waivers of discharge for pregnancy. They also changed the enlistment rules so that women with children were no longer automatically excluded from entering the service. The military was experiencing a loss of their enlisted women annually to pregnancy and parenthood. To alleviate this the Department of Defense instructed the services to develop and implement policies of voluntary separation for pregnancy and parenthood. Of course, the powers that be objected with concerns about availability for deployment and potential loss of duty time, but they had to comply by 1975. Military women instigated litigation on this issue in the courts. In 1976 the Second District Court ruled that a Marine Corps regulation requiring the discharge of a pregnant woman Marine violated the Fifth Amendment due process clause because it set up an irrefutable presumption that any pregnant woman in uniform was permanently unfit for duty. Finally in the late 1970's, shortly after the decision was made to permit women who became pregnant to remain in the military, maternity uniforms were developed by each service.[31]

---

31 Military Women and Pregnancy – Aug.com, " Pregnancy Discrimination," userpages.aug.com/captbarb/pregnancy.html

CHAPTER NINE

Before Mary said her goodbyes, I remember both of us going to shopping malls so she could buy baby clothes. She seemed so happy to be having this child with Jack. One day instead of taking the city bus, we went with Jack's roommate, Pete, the one who stayed for just a short time at our introductory party.

Pete brought his beautiful 1967 corvette convertible to El Paso and drove it whenever he had the chance. He decided it was fine for Mary and me to ride to the mall with him one beautiful warm sunny September afternoon. I remember how funny it was for the three of us to fit into that small two-seater. Mary said she would straddle the center between the two seats where the gear box was located. What a ride! Pete had some things to buy at a hardware store, so Mary said she would run into the nearby clothing store while I tagged along with Pete. I believe she was trying to get me to take notice of him before she left, as I later found out her fondness for Charlie and our relationship was waning.

Pete grasped my hand in his as we approached the store's entrance and immediately, I felt an electric shock. I don't know if he felt it as well. I remember thinking how strange. Suddenly, I sensed it was a paranormal phenomenon or a signal to let me know we were to be paired for life. His strong hand grip while guiding me into the store felt so comforting. Our friendship and fondness for each other grew quickly after that ride to the mall.

He explained one evening when we had gone out to dinner that he almost didn't get to graduate because he was missing one credit when his draft number was called up. He was "biting bullets" trying to get his diploma in Industrial Design from the University of Illinois before going to the induction center.

Fortunately, after going before a board of professors, he did get that last credit needed for graduation.

When WWI and WWII were pending, the U.S. Congress passed selective service acts that gave the president the authority to draft men into the military. Throughout the wars in Korea and Vietnam, several selective service acts were also passed. During these various periods of conscription, a classification system was used to determine eligibility. During the Korean and Vietnam eras, the system comprised 21 classifications.[32]

Men who were classified 1-A were deemed available for unrestricted military service. A 1-A classification meant that they could be drafted whenever needed. Anyone registered for the draft was classified 1-H.[33]

The 4-F classification indicated that the man was unacceptable for military service due to his inability to meet physical, mental, or moral standards. Individuals with mental or physical disabilities were excluded from the draft. The 4-G classification exempted individuals due to the death of a sibling or parent while serving in the U.S. armed forces or who had a parent or sibling listed as captured or missing in action.[34]

Since its inception in the 1860's, the idea of a military draft or conscription has generated much debate and resistance up to and including protests and "draft dodging." Its legality and constitutionality have been challenged all the way up to the Supreme Court. Conscription, or "the draft," is a means for the United States military to call up additional troops when needed for national defense.[35]

Congress passed the Selective Service Act in May 1917. Initially, all men ages 21 to 30 were required to register for selective service. However, the Act was later revised to include men from

---

32 Douglas Hawk, "U.S. Military Draft Classification in the 1950's & 1960's," https://classroom.com>us-military-draft
33 As above
34 As above
35 Douglas Hawk, "U.S. Military Draft Classification in the 1950's & 1960's," https://classroom.com>us-military-draft

the ages of 18 to 45. Also, there was a significant difference in the 1917 acts and the Civil War acts: Potential draftees could not hire substitutes to fight in their place.[36]

The draft during Vietnam contained the birth date September 14. That meant all men born on September 14 were first in line to be drafted into the military. Furthermore, after the birth dates were drawn, 26 letters of the alphabet were drawn. J was drawn first, and V was drawn last. Therefore, a man with the name Johnson would be called before a man with the last name Vickers.[37]

The draft process sparked protests, and many young men, as I mentioned before, fled the country instead of reporting for duty. Others, like the famous heavy weight boxing champion, Muhammad Ali, were arrested and faced trial for draft evasion. Some young men received student deferments to complete their educations, but even that process caused controversy, because some saw it as favoring men from wealthier families who could afford college. "If you got the dough, you don't have to go."[38]

Since the first Conscription Acts of the Civil War, there has been a contention that the draft is unconstitutional and illegal. Most notably, detractors use the 13th Amendment to support this argument. It states that "Neither slavery nor involuntary servitude, except as a punishment for crime whereof the party shall have been duly convicted, shall exist within the United States, or any place subject to their jurisdiction." However, in the case of Arver vs. the United States, the Supreme court upheld the constitutionality of the draft, because the constitution gave Congress the power to raise armies, and conscription had been used in colonial America as well as in England.[39]

---

36 As above
37 As above
38 As above
39 Douglas Hawk, "U.S. Military Draft Classification in the 1950's & 1960's," https://classroom.com>us-military-draft

In 1980, President Jimmy Carter reestablished the Selective Service System. Although this was done during peacetime, the purpose was "to provide a hedge against unforeseen threats." Currently by law, all men between the ages of 18 and 25 are required to register for Selective Service within 30 days of their 18th birthday, before or after. This includes cadets at the Merchant Marine Academy, ROTC students, people who left active-duty armed forces before the age of 26, National Guardsmen and Reservists who are currently not on active duty and Civil Air Patrol members. Some non-citizens are also required to register if living in the United States. These include resident aliens, seasonal agricultural workers, illegal aliens, refugees, asylum seekers and dual nationals. Women do not have to register because Selective Service law specifies "male persons."[40]

---

[40] https://www.upi,com>Top>News>2020/01/23/On-This-Day-Jimmy-Carter-revives-selective-service/9541579659761

CHAPTER TEN

I wrote letters to Charlie usually twice a week. My OR course required a lot of studying, so I used my limited spare time for writing and reading our correspondence. I did notice Charlie's letters were coming less frequently which bothered me somewhat. One letter he wrote really had me confused. He told me to go out and party or have a good time with friends, especially since I loved parties so much. He didn't want me to just stay at home alone during that year long waiting period. Did he not know me well enough to remember I didn't even like parties? I wasn't into the social scene much and staying by myself on weekends was not a problem for me. I didn't even like to drink or dance, as I mentioned before. I enjoyed being by myself.

I showed this letter to Pete when he stopped in to say hello one evening as I wanted his reaction.

His immediate response was, "He's playing around! He wants you to do the same, so he doesn't feel guilty! What an ass! I wondered what you ever saw in him! He's a baby! Get rid of him!"

His counsel was appreciated. But I decided to think about this relationship for a few days before sending another letter. Within two days the answer was clear. I received a call from the San Antonio jewelry store where Charlie purchased my engagement ring. They said they hadn't received a payment for over a month and, not being able to reach him, they requested I either send the monthly payments or return the ring.

My God! So, his interest and devotion were now over? I was sickened but also so angry that I packaged up the ring the next day and returned it. Suddenly I was free! Immediately, I thought of Kathy, my friend from nursing school. I wondered if she was free from her despicable husband, Tim. Fortunately, Charlie and I had not taken those vows of marriage. Sadly, as I mentioned before, I didn't really expect him to return alive from Vietnam, and now it didn't concern me any longer.

I told Mary about the letter, and she did not react as I thought she would. She expressed no surprise. So, I asked, "Did you know he was being unfaithful over there in Da Nang?"

Directing her gaze into my eyes, she admitted she was aware of his philandering.

"When did you know?" I questioned.

"About a month ago, Karen told me. Mike mentioned it in one of his letters. She told me not to tell you. Sorry, Susan. I didn't want this to hurt you which is why I decided to send you off with Pete that day we went shopping. I think he is good for you. Charlie is too immature, and I could tell Pete really likes you, and you seem to really enjoy his company."

Slowly after taking a deep breath, I answered, "Well thanks for thinking about my feelings, Mary. I am glad the truth is out, and I can move on now. No more constraints. The "Dear John letter" was reversed wasn't it." We both laughed.

While the exact origins of the phrase "dear John" are unknown, the most likely origin dates to the 1862 poem *No, thank you, John* by Christina Rossetti. More specifically, the female protagonist Alice Vavasor in Anthony Trollope's 1864 novel 'Can Your Forgive Her', composes a letter to her soon to be spurned lover John Grey. It is commonly believed to have been coined by Americans during WWII. "John" was the most popular and common baby name for boys in America every single year from 1880 through 1923. Large numbers of American troops were stationed overseas for many months or years. As time passed many of their wives or girlfriends decided to begin relationships with new men, rather than to wait for the soldiers to return.[41]

---

41 Wikipedia, "Dear John Letter," https://en.wikipedia.org>wiki>Dear_John_letter

"This is so interesting. I am learning so much as I listen to you tell about your life back in the 1970's."

After finishing a little dusting in my room, she continued, "I have to get back to work now, but tomorrow is my day off. Do you mind if I come to visit you? I want to hear the rest of your life story!" Cyndi voiced enthusiastically.

Smiling I said, "Yes dear. If I'm still here tomorrow, I would love to reiterate my saga to a willing recipient."

CHAPTER ELEVEN

"Good morning Mrs. Farwell. It's such a nice day. May I take you out to the garden? There I can listen again to your wonderful story," Cyndi said, after knocking and peeking through my door that was slightly ajar. "I also brought a lunch basket for us."

"What a nice gesture. That would be wonderful to sit outside under the beautiful big oak tree that I admire each day and enjoy the wonderful lunch you prepared. That is, if you don't mind spending your afternoon with an old lady," I shyly stated with a tear in my eye.

"Let me think about where I left off. Oh yes. I was talking about Charlie, I believe," as I took a bite of a delicious tuna sandwich.

I never felt remorse or sadness about the breakup with Charlie. In fact, I didn't even know if he was aware that I returned his ring to the jeweler.

I spent more and more time with Pete, especially after Mary was discharged, and I had no other roommate for the remaining time in El Paso. My grades were good, as I continued to study diligently, and the time I spent with Pete was fun and relaxing. I did notice he had very few friends, and he soon left the apartment he once shared with Mary's husband, Jack, and two others. Pete moved into another apartment in the complex with two other guys after Jack left to go to his next duty station. It pleased me that he seemed more compatible with them.

Enlistees wanted to live off post, but to afford that option they needed to share the expense with several guys, making for very cramped quarters.

His dream, after leaving the military, was to pursue a career in design. He told me he had been fortunate to get a well-paying design job just three months after getting his degree. But his excitement was reigned in with the draft. His plan was to return to that company when he was discharged in the next few months. He showed me his art portfolio one evening, and I was hugely impressed with his artistic talent and was certain he would be quite successful.

In fact, one drawing he showed me actually startled me! During his sophomore year, one of his professors instructed the students to design a plaque for the winner of an athletic swimming event. The name of that recipient was to be included in the design, as well. When I looked at the name written on the base of the plaque drawing, I noticed it was my middle name and my last name! Pete didn't even know my middle name, so when I told him this he was also shocked! He said he chose those two names for balance. I think we both had chills! Another paranormal phenomenon?

I will never forget our first embrace and kiss. After taking me to dinner on a December evening , he said he wanted to drive me to a beautiful spot in the Franklin Mountains. I suspected he had taken several girls up this road to his favorite make-out destination many times in the past. He was quite handsome, and I knew several of the nurses in the complex really wanted his attention.

He had removed the fiberglass top of his corvette before we left. When we finally stopped at his favorite spot after maneuvering many mountain curves, he took a blanket out of the trunk and placed it on the ground several yards from the road. We stood for a moment to view the colorful lights of the city. The night air gave me a chill, so he took off his jacket and wrapped it around me while enclosing me against his chest. He then kissed me sending chills up my spine. I never felt that with the other guys I had dated, including Charlie. That special bond I felt when we clasped our hands together at the shopping mall only intensified after that first kiss on this beautiful starry night as I felt the strength of his arms enveloping me.

Pete loved his corvette, and at least once a week, I would see him outside my apartment window, washing and waxing every inch of that car. He looked so sexy wearing his unlaced combat boots, a pair of old white army medical trousers that he had cut into shorts, and shirtless! Wow! Many girls didn't appreciate that "hairy chest look." But I did! Besides his cute attire, he had the body of superman! He was often asked if he worked out and always replied, "No, I was born this way." Which was true. He inherited his physique from his grandfather.

One Saturday afternoon, when Pete was cleaning that beautiful car, I went outside, sat in the window seat of my apartment, and watched him work. At first, he wasn't aware I was there. But, within a few minutes, he looked up, smiled, and came over to sit with me. He said he needed a little break.

"How are you able to keep that long hair," I asked as his curly auburn waves blew in the warm breeze. "I thought there were strict rules about that."

He smiled, showing those great dimples, and said, "Dippity Doo."

We laughed. Suddenly, he looked at me closely and said, "Do you know how beautiful you are? Those eyes! Wow! Where did you get those green eyes?"

I didn't blush, but I loved hearing these words from him.

"My great uncle in Denmark on my grandmother's side of the family had green eyes. So, I guess I got them from him. I don't know anyone else in the family who has green eyes. My grandfather and grandmother came over from Aalborg when they were young," I answered.

"Wow! I thank him for you! You know only 2% of the world population has green eyes. You should feel incredibly special."

"Thanks," I answered somewhat shyly.

Placing his arm around my shoulder he said, "May I tell you something? I love you, Susan."

"No way! You hardly know me. How many times have we gone out together? Not many, maybe five or so," I replied, questioning his feelings.

"I don't need more time to know I love you. I have never met anyone like you. I've dated plenty of women, and you are in a category by yourself. Do you know that?" he asked while continuing to hold me close.

"I don't know what you mean."

"How many guys have you dated who told you they loved you? Seriously! And how old are you? Not even twenty-two yet! I'm sure quite a few, am I right? This puts you in a category by yourself," he continued.

He gave me a quick peck on the cheek and stood up to finish waxing his car.

"I am serious about what I said. After all, you met my parents. Only one other girlfriend has met them. So, you should feel privileged. Plus, they really like you, and they didn't like her," he winked and smiled, showing off those dimples.

He further added, "I only have a few more months before my discharge papers come through, and then I'll be going back home to live. I want to get my position back that I told you about in industrial design. But I promise I will come to see you wherever you are stationed. I don't like thinking about us being separated."

I suddenly thought back to one particular day when we walked together from the apartments to the hospital early one morning for our assigned duties.....me in the OR and Pete on the Psychiatric ward where he was in charge as a specialist 5. I read him a letter I had received from mom. She wrote that grandfather had died. This was the most heart wrenching letter I received during my tour of duty. Thankfully, apparently he didn't suffer. He was with my mom's oldest sister then, and after Thanksgiving dinner he sat in his favorite rocking chair to take a short nap. He never woke up! The remorse I felt for not saying goodbye with a hug and kiss for him when I left home to join the Army was so painful. Pete gave me such comfort at that difficult time. I think this was when I realized I loved him.

Fortunately, he didn't ask me to marry him when he was discharged, but I knew I wanted him in my life. Once again, my mind took me back to that day he grasped my hand, leading me into that store at the mall. Something strange in the cosmos had happened then. I genuinely believed we were meant to be together.

CHAPTER TWELVE

My spirituality has been strong as far back into my childhood as I can remember. I mentioned that it was important for my mother to read the Bible to us during our lunch break from school, and we had to say our prayers each night before going to bed. But, for me there was more.

At church, even when only five years old or so, I remember wiping tears from my face while listening to the pastor's sermons. I didn't always know what he was trying to teach us or preach to us. But I felt an emotional connection in that beautiful house of God, feelings I still can't fully describe, while trying to sit up straight in that large pew. I remember a few times my younger brother, Jim, would lean over and whisper, "What are you crying about?" I felt somewhat embarrassed and didn't have an answer for him. I loved the church interior and the picture of Christ on the wall at the church narthex or entrance. I felt comforted by that huge painting, even though His eyes looked sad to me. I believed He would protect me. Possibly because I didn't receive that affection and love from my mother, I needed that solace from within the church confines.

I read my little Bible from the Old Testament through to the end of the New Testament two or three times when I was a child, even though much of it I didn't understand. The book of Revelations scared me then and still does.

I felt God spoke to me often throughout my life. By the age of twelve, I knew that I would never have children. That thought just came to me one day. At the age of eleven and possibly even earlier, I knew I would have a problem with my appendix sometime in the future. By the age of fourteen my appendix had indeed ruptured. Three days later I was in the hospital. I prayed to God that if he let me live, I would become a nurse. After a slow recovery, I had forgotten that promise. I decided I wanted to be an artist. But my promise to God was fulfilled, despite the direction I wanted to take in my career. Nursing was the route chosen for me.

I studied several different religions during my adult life, and I concluded that we come into this world with a blueprint. Our life choices are determined prior to birth. We can't deviate from that given pathway even if we try. We are here to learn lessons before passing out of this world. Some pastor friends didn't agree with my notions obviously, but none of us are sure about the true meaning of life on earth and the hereafter.

So, my feeling about this connection to Pete was amplified by my spiritual beliefs.

"How interesting! I don't always make it to church each Sunday, but I do believe in God. Many of my friends don't though. In fact lots of them are atheists! They think I am crazy to believe in the existence of God," Cyndi replied with her head hanging low.

"Everyone must reach their own conclusion about religion, faith, and God," I replied.

CHAPTER THIRTEEN

One late December morning, just before the holidays, my classmates and I sat across from one another at this long table waiting with great anticipation for our OR course instructor to enter the room. When she finally arrived, she handed each of us an envelope. Our course was completed, and this envelope contained orders for our new assignment or duty station. As each of us looked at one another, we could almost feel the collective apprehension.

When I slowly opened the envelope, I was surprised I didn't receive orders for Vietnam. Mentally I prepared myself for this assignment because with the MOS of operating room nurse, I knew we were desperately needed over there. Also, when I was still engaged to Charlie, I thought I wanted to be there with him. But I learned of many combat soldiers as well as medical staff suffering with attacks of anxiety and flashbacks after returning to the states. This mental condition was not given a label until five years later in 1980 after the war ended. The condition became known as PTSD (post-traumatic stress syndrome). So, thinking back on my first choice, I was appreciative of my new duty station, which would probably not change before I finished my two-year commitment.

Surprisingly, this duty station was Denver! I had mixed feelings about returning home, but since five months had passed, I was certain mom needed me nearby to help with her care. I thought possibly her surgeon had something to do with my military assignment. He knew people in "high places."

I was provided with a second story, furnished two-bedroom apartment located in the officer's quarters or quadrangle. There were four red brick apartment buildings facing each other to form a square. My rent was only six dollars a month. I remember being shocked at this price, especially since the furnishings were nice. The view from my living room looking down into the center of the square was quite pretty with the manicured shrubbery and cement walkways meandering through the lush green lawn. Benches had been placed along the walkways for us to sit outside and enjoy the fragrances of the blooming flowers or just for outside relaxation.

From my apartment it was just a short walk to the hospital across the main throughfare, not far from the Army Post entrance which was always guarded. I received a warm welcome from my boss, a nurse with the rank of lieutenant colonel, as well as the rest of the OR staff which was about 60. I probably had the lowest rank among the officers, being a second lieutenant with a gold bar insignia, but that didn't bother me. Within a few months I received my silver bar as a first lieutenant. If I had reenlisted for another tour of duty after my two-year commitment, I would have become a captain probably six months later. I was told rank was achieved quickly during war time.

I was immediately assigned to night shift duty after getting a two- week orientation which was the norm for a new member of the staff. I remember having the "graveyard" shift (12 midnight to 8 A.M.) when I became a new graduate nurse. The night shift did not go well with my biorhythms, but I learned to adjust and developed an adequate sleeping schedule after a while.

The hospital was one of the larger Army hospitals in the states, with orthopedics being one of the main surgical specialties. As a tertiary hospital, which is a highly specialized care center for performing advanced, complex procedures and treatments by medical specialists, our operating suites stayed busy. There were twelve of these suites, and the larger ones for major surgeries had huge windows which impressed me. The hospital was located near the airport, and I remember during one case, the surgeons left their positions at the operating table to watch the newly designed huge 747 jets land! The only person in charge of the sedated patient was the anesthesiologist! But soon the OR staff resumed their collective responsibilities, and the surgical case resumed.

After working for a year on a surgical ward prior to my enlistment, I found the move to the OR so different. No longer did I have any communication with patients, except when instructing them to move from the gurney onto the cold operating room table. Within minutes they were sedated, then intubated, if necessary, and the case was started. I missed that personal one on one contact with them.

During the night shift, the only cases were those urgent surgeries called up from the ER (emergency room). As a new employee this slower shift was to aid in the transition and preparation to the more hectic schedules during the day. I thought I would be okay with that decision, but it turned out not to be quite what I expected.

I would leave my apartment around 11:30 P.M. (2330 hrs.) and walk across the street and up the block to the hospital. I was never frightened because the streetlamps provided enough light, and the MPs (military police) patrolled the area all the time. I was happy to wear my "civilian clothes" including bellbottoms (the fad back in the 70's) to work.

Each staff member had been assigned to a locker in the dressing rooms. Fortunately, they were segregated. I would change into scrubs, hat, or head cover, and my OR shoes to be ready for whatever came up. I had one corpsman assigned with me. So, if we had a case called in, we would pull the required instruments, autoclave them, and set up the suite for the surgeon(s) arrival. Usually I scrubbed on the case, which meant I was standing at the OR table, handing the instruments to the surgeon(s) as needed. The circulator would not have to be gowned up in sterile clothing because that person would gather any supplies needed such as extra suture. If any equipment had to be setup, that was their assignment as well.

The corpsman initially assigned to work with me was a specialist 7, or sergeant. He was considered a "lifer" and had plans to put in at least 20 years of service. He oversaw the corpsmen of lesser ranking, while a specialist 8 was in command of all of them in our OR. I felt comforted knowing that I would spend my first few weeks on the night shift with a very experienced corpsman.

Thinking back, I recall having always worked diligently with any task or assignment given to me. Since taking my first job at the age of sixteen, working in an all-women's nursing home, the managers started me off cleaning the women's bathrooms. There were nineteen of them. Learning that the ladies were pleased with my cleaning skills, I was soon responsible for cleaning the dayroom as well. Within a few months, I was assigned to help the cooks with table settings and serving. Eventually I was preparing light meals on weekends when the cooks were off duty. I was told I learned quickly and worked efficiently. If I found any idle time, I made good use of that time by cleaning and organizing the work areas. When I became a nurse, I made sure I found time to listen to the patients' fears and concerns as well. I never wasted my working hours with idle gossip or just sitting around doing nothing productive. I made sure I earned my hourly pay!

Without having patients to talk to in the OR, I found cleaning helped pass the time when we weren't doing any cases. Occasionally the on-call surgeon would come up to say hello and sometimes spend the night sleeping on the sofa in the breakroom. I was responsible for giving the day crew a report of the events of the night and any new cases that might have been added at the end of their schedule.

One morning I remember telling the oncoming crew that the on-call surgeon had spent the night in the OR, sleeping in the lounge. I heard a roar of laughter from the day staff. I didn't understand why until one of the nurses told me the surgeons only came to the OR to sleep because a new cute lieutenant had arrived. I blushed!

One night when it seemed slow and no cases were expected, I went into the largest suite used for open heart surgeries. I looked out through one of the massive windows at the brightly illuminated full moon sky. It was so pretty. While taking in this serene beauty, I thought I heard footsteps.

"Beautiful night isn't it?" Initially startled, I quickly turned to see who was standing behind me.

"Forgive me if I frightened you. My name is Larry, and I am on call tonight. I just came from the ER, and it is slow down there, too. So, I really doubt we will have any work tonight, I am happy to report," he stated in a calming voice.

"Wonderful!" I could use a slow night as I didn't get enough sleep. This night shift doesn't agree with me," I said, smiling after introducing myself.

He admitted, "I knew who you were. Your name has been floating around this hospital ever since you arrived. A month ago, right?"

"My goodness! Yes, that is why I am stuck on this graveyard shift right now. Why does everyone know me?" I inquired.

"You don't know? You are the best-looking thing to come through this hospital's doors for quite a while now, and I have been here almost a year."

I felt embarrassed and yet flattered by his comment, but also somewhat nervous. Here I was in a large operating room suite, lit only by the full moon shining through the large window with a stranger standing too close for comfort and no corpsman in sight. I found myself slowly backing away as I headed towards the door while he continued with light conversation. Fortunately, he received a page and had to go down to one of the wards to see a patient.

When I quickly returned to the breakroom, I asked the corpsman how this physician happened to find me in that room, and he said, "I told him you were back there somewhere."

"Thanks for that! He startled me! Don't do it again!" I scolded.

On quite nights when all the cleaning I could find to do was finished, I did sit in the breakroom with the sergeant. Initially, our conversations were about our personal lives, such as families and where we lived, etc.. Rarely did we talk about this war and the casualties.

But one night, he was sitting in the chair facing the door while I was sitting on the lounge sofa next to his chair. After giving me a strange smile, he opened the conversation with the topic of sex. He wanted to know if I was engaged and how many boyfriends I had in the past. At first, I answered his questions, but then he asked how I felt about sexual activity with older men. He was 20 years my senior. I knew where his questions were leading and immediately, I instinctively crossed my legs. I felt boxed in and frightened! I wanted that phone to ring from the ER. Where was the on-call doctor now? I knew this man could get an Article 15 for taking advantage of me, but with his queries, he wanted to know how far he could go with me.

"Stop! This conversation is over," I said sharply.

I don't know where I got the courage to say that, but he backed off and left the room.

I reported what occurred the next morning to the Lt. Colonel. She listened intently while taking notes and said she would let his commanding officer know what happened then get back to me as soon as possible.

Well, I didn't hear back from her but instead heard from the NCO. He asked to speak to me in the linen supply room of all places. Corpsman were coming in and out, getting their scrubs while we spoke. Interesting I thought. What about privacy? I immediately thought this location for our conversation was deliberate! The strategy was that I would become reluctant to explain what really occurred that night since corpsmen were able to listen to our conversation. My word! The NCO didn't want to hear the truth!

But, after bravely telling what transpired with that sexual innuendo, the NCO said, "This man has been here for a long time, and no accusation such as this has ever been brought forward before. I will remove him from the night shift to ease your concern. But, lieutenant, might I suggest since you are an attractive young woman, you stop wearing scrub dresses and change into scrub pants when you arrive for duty in the future."

So, I was the guilty party? Not him! I had just received a rude awakening into this world where I now worked. I honestly thought the sergeant would get a reprimand of some kind. It never happened!

An Article 15 of the Uniform Code of Military Justice allows for the commanding officer to decide the innocence or guilt, then administer the punishment to the offender, if necessary, when a military member gets into trouble for a minor offense that does not require a judicial hearing. An Article 15 hearing is less formal than a court-martial.[42]

Knowing I had to continue to work with this man in the future, I decided to remain quiet and hope that I never found myself in this kind of position again. Also, as requested, I stopped wearing scrub dresses.

---

42 Stewart Smith, "What is an Article 15?" www.thebalancecareers.com/what-is-an-article-15-3354210 updated July 27, 2020

CHAPTER FOURTEEN

Not long after that dreadful experience, I was finally assigned to work on the day shift. I guess they wanted to keep an eye on me and prevent this from happening again.

"How are you doing, Susan?" Bette asked after I had just finished a short case.

"How to make friends and influence people is not going so well for me, I guess."

"Don't worry about it. You will be here for a long while and time heals all wounds. Just remember that," she smiled while giving me a strong pat on my back.

"Listen, do you have any plans this evening?" she suddenly asked.

"No, not really. I don't really like going to the officer's club. Why?" I asked.

"If you haven't noticed, I have the apartment just below you. Why don't I stop up, and we can have a few beers together? It might just erase some of that stress you seem to be having right now."

"Wow! Is it that noticeable?" I asked.

"It's okay, you just need to dry your feet," she replied.

Bette and I hit it off the first day I arrived. She was a captain and planned to make a career of Army life. She was assigned to my orientation for the two weeks before I was pushed off to night duty. I learned a lot from her and found her to be a skilled operating room nurse. I hadn't made any friends yet, especially since I was working nights and slept during the day, so I accepted her invitation to stop by my place that evening.

The only thing I had in the kitchen to eat was a Tupperware bowl full of chocolate chip cookies I had made a few days earlier. I hadn't been to the PX (post exchange) for weeks to get groceries. I just ate peanut butter crackers from the dispensing machine in our breakroom and drank a soda while at work. I was too tired when I came home to do anything but sleep. So fortunately, I was glad Bette came with two beers when she knocked at my door. She brought a few music albums as well.

I wasn't a beer drinker, but I accepted her kind gesture and slowly sipped my can of Coors. We sat on the floor in front of the stereo console, and she opened the albums to show me her favorite music. I don't remember what songs she played, but the sound was comforting and calming. I was glad it wasn't hard rock music.

Suddenly, Bette placed her hand over mine and looking straight into my eyes said, "Susan, I really like you."

Oh no! Here it comes again, only this time with the wrong gender, I thought to myself. Maybe my spurning the gestures of the sergeant made her think I didn't prefer men. I didn't want to hurt her feelings, as she had been so nice and helpful to me at work, but I had to terminate her gestures immediately! I didn't even know of same sex relationships until I was a student nurse. There was a rumor that the president of the senior class was a lesbian, but I didn't even know what that meant and was told by some of my classmates that I was very naive.

Quickly I said, "Thanks Bette, but I am sorry this won't work. I have a boyfriend in Illinois."

That sounded so trite, but I didn't know what else to say to her, and it was the truth. I was expecting to hear from Pete any day.

I think she felt slightly embarrassed as well. She took the record from the stereo, packed up her albums and told me goodbye. Fortunately, we didn't have to work on the same cases in surgery, and we cordially exchanged greetings when passing through the hallways. I had no further concerns about her. I accepted her sexual preference, but it was not mine.

CHAPTER FIFTEEN

The call from Pete was too late in coming, especially after the two encounters I had with fellow employees. My phone service hadn't been set up yet, so I decided I would walk across the street, and call Pete from the phone in the day room of the BOQ (Bachelor Officer's Quarters) building.

This long red brick building housed officers who were having extensive medical treatments or procedures along with physical rehabilitation for their combat injuries. Each officer had a small room with an attached bathroom. I had never been in this building before, but I remember someone told me that until my phone was operable, I could use the phone in this building.

Fortunately, no one was sitting in this large room when I entered, so I sat in the chair by the phone to make my call. Pete didn't want to pay for a phone in his apartment, but he said I could reach him at work anytime. After two rings, I was glad to hear his voice.

"Hi, when do you plan to come visit?" I eagerly asked.

"Gosh, Susan, I can't afford to come see you right now."

"It isn't that expensive, is it?" I questioned.

"Hey! I can't even afford to buy new tires for my corvette, so how am I going to find the money to visit you. Don't get me wrong; I want to come as soon as I can. I really miss you, but I just can't afford it right now. Sorry," he replied somewhat reluctantly.

While we were talking, I noticed a guy passing by with a load of laundry, apparently on his way to the washing machines in the basement. He stopped briefly to look my way. It bothered me since I wanted to have a private conversation, so I was glad when he disappeared. After a few minutes he was back, and again he stopped as if he wanted to overhear my conversation. The nerve of him! I believe I gave him a stern glare, but this time I realized it was fruitless to discuss Pete's future visit, so we said our goodbyes. The acoustics must have been quite loud because this guy, who I noticed had a limp, came back up the hall from his room before I had a chance to get up out of the chair.

"Excuse me," he said while approaching me.

"My name is Ken. I am sorry for eavesdropping on your conversation, but it sounded like it wasn't going well. Was that your boyfriend?" he asked.

Oh my! Who is this pushy guy anyway, I wondered?

Not to be rude, I replied, "Yes, I was hoping he could come visit me soon. I just transferred here, and he was discharged a few months ago. I thought he would be able to find the time to come out especially since the weather is getting warmer."

"That's too bad," he said solemnly.

"Do you live here?" I asked while wanting to return to my apartment.

"Yes, my room is just down the hall. You may have noticed I am in the process of doing my laundry," he sheepishly laughed. "Are you a nurse? You said you recently transferred here."

"I should introduce myself, too. My name is Susan. Fitzsimons is my permanent duty station probably for the next year and a half when I will be finished with my two-year commitment," I replied.

Smiling, he said, "I haven't seen you on the orthopedics ward, so you must work in a different department."

"I work in the OR. That was the MOS I wanted when I signed up. Have you been a patient on the ortho ward? I notice you have a limp," I commented, while trying to detect any deformities in his legs.

"Yes, I was wounded in Vietnam about six months ago and since Fitzsimons is the closest military hospital to my hometown, I was sent here for rehab. Fortunately, it is an excellent facility for orthopedic issues," he answered.

"Oh, I am so sorry. I hope you recover soon. Well, I should be getting back to my place." I wanted to end these pleasantries to spend the rest of my day sulking after my disappointing phone call with Pete.

"Listen, since you haven't been here long, I assume you don't know your way around yet. I know a great place that serves a tasty Denver omelet. Would you like to join me for a light supper?" he shyly asked.

I wasn't ready for company, but then I thought why not.

"Sure! If you could see into my kitchen cupboards, you would ask yourself, 'Is ketchup all she eats?'" We both laughed.

He quickly responded, "Meet me here in an hour. Will that work for you?"

"Absolutely. It won't take me long to get ready. I will see you soon. And thanks. I am really hungry," I replied, thinking he seemed like a nice guy, and I felt I could easily forgive him for what started as a rude interruption at first.

An omelet meant casual dining, so getting ready was quick and easy. I would just slip on my favorite pair of maroon colored bell bottoms and my lacy white blouse. My sandals would be appropriate, too.

We were both prompt. He was wearing jeans and cowboy boots. I wasn't keen on those boots, but he said he lived near this area, so I decided he was a rancher's son. His hair was quite short after seeing Pete's long curly dark hair. The blond color made it appear even shorter. He said he couldn't stand to have his hair grow over his ears, so he had it trimmed often.

He led me outside, and there at the curb was this beautiful pristine red corvette.

"Wow, nice car! Is that yours?" I asked.

"You like it? I promise to give you a safe ride. I bought this after my injury to help me maintain some cool headedness during the rehabilitation process, which I understand will take some time. I love driving it. It helps me unwind," he somewhat reluctantly replied.

I sensed he was a very proud person. His demeanor showed great confidence, even though he struggled with his walking at times.

The restaurant was inside one of the new hotels not far from the post. He selected a booth for us. After we sat down across from each other, I immediately noticed a large ring on his right index finger.

"Is that your class ring?" I asked.

"Yes, it is. I am not really into wearing rings as they bother me when I work on my car. But I am not doing much of that now, so this car better behave for quite a long time," he laughed.

"My, I have never seen one that large. Where did you go to school?"

"West Point," he answered hesitantly so as not to appear braggadocious.

Immediately, I liked his humbleness. I was sure, if I hadn't asked, he would not have ventured to tell me. A few minutes later our omelets arrived and being famished, I didn't ask him any further personal questions. The evening went by quickly, and after arriving back at the post, we said our goodbyes. I wasn't sure if I would ever see him again, but our supper "date" helped me forget the disappointing call with Pete.

"Mrs. Farwell. I wish I had as many boyfriends as you had when you were young," Cyndi interjected.

Smiling, I replied, "You probably won't as I continue with my story. If you have a friend who truly cares for you and loves you dearly, be happy with that satisfaction."

I continued once again.

CHAPTER SIXTEEN

I had a dear friend from high school, Nancy, who I felt would be very compatible with Ken. She graduated a year ahead of me. She was so sweet and cute, and she lived on a small farm a few miles from my home. Her dad reminded me of Ken, with his blond hair, blue eyes, and even similar jesters. We discussed her decision to enter nursing school. I knew she would do well and be an excellent nurse. She had the required attributes of compassion and caring that were so important. When I mentioned him to her, she said she would meet him since she currently wasn't dating anyone.

I loved setting friends up on blind date as I always thought I could match them up well. It worked! They arranged to meet, and I was excited for them. I hadn't talked to either one of them for a week or two after that. I was too upset about Pete's seemingly lack of interest in flying out to see me. We had several more conversations about this, and I decided I had had enough. I wasn't going to beg him to come, so I broke up with him. I told him I wanted to see other people. He sounded sad, but he said he was so busy with new design creations. He didn't have time for anything else. My thought that we were meant to be together was waning.

I remember going to the officer's club with a new nursing friend, Katie. She was the head nurse on the orthopedic ward. She also lived in the same building as I, but on the first floor across from Bette. Before meeting her, I noticed many guys would just appear at her door and I wondered who they were.

After we greeted each other coming home from work one day, I asked her about them.

Laughing she replied, "Oh, it isn't a 'menage a trois' if that's what you were thinking. They are my patients."

"Oh, forgive me for being nosy. They seem to come around a lot, so your therapeutic skills must be working," I smiled.

"I do try to get them out of the hospital as much as I can. I also take as many as will fit into my car to church every Sunday," she added.

"Oh, that is wonderful, Katie," I stated.

She was a farm girl from South Dakota. She couldn't wait to get back home to see her boyfriend, she said. But she had committed to four years in the Army since they paid for her college education just like Mary and the dietician Kelly. It was a great recruiting tactic, especially during war time when nurses were highly needed as well as "manpower" in general. Many guys were in ROTC (Reserve Officers' Training Corps). They were given scholarships for their education followed by military commitments as officers.

Katie and I found time to get together, usually for lunch on weekends. She didn't like the bar scene either. But, for whatever reason, we did go to the club one night. As clubs go, it was very noisy and smokey. We were outnumbered, of course, and in a nearby room there was a pool table, with several guys standing around laughing and trying their best to make pocket shots with their pool cues. I recall one guy looked immediately at the entrance when we walked through the door. He must have been looking for someone. But shortly after that he left the game and came to where we were sitting. Katie didn't need an introduction. She introduced him to me as he too was one of her patients.

"Hi, Paul. You appear to be doing well. This is my friend Susan. Susan, this is Paul," she said somewhat reluctantly.

With slurred words, he leaned into me and with that glassy glaze and said, "Well, from what part of the Universe did you pop out from?"

Because of his cigarette and alcohol breath, I could hardly reply. It made me a little nauseous. Beyond that introduction, though he was very handsome and reminded me somewhat of Pete, except his build was slender. We did carry on a conversation for a while after Katie excused herself to go back home. I thought to myself, don't leave me here with him, but she had to be up early the next day.

When I tried to tell him it was extremely late, about 0100, he said he wanted to take me for a ride on his motorcycle. My apartment was just a block away, so I thought he could take me there without any difficulty. I didn't want to be involved in a crash with this drunk driver.

Instead, however, he took me around the block several times. I was really concerned because when he hopped onto his bike, I noticed he had a prothesis on his left lower leg. He was an amputee! Orthopedics was one area of nursing that did not interest me, but I appreciated Katie's commitment and involvement with this medical specialty.

"Is it painful?" I asked, not knowing how or even if I should broach the subject.

"Oh, it's nothing. I'm used to it now. I just have to learn to do things differently. It does makes me angry to be a 'cripple' though."

My nurse persona was starting to come out as I asked, "This depression is causing you to drink too much. Am I right?"

"Nah, I love a good party!" he answered, dismissing my query.

Luckily, there were no mishaps, and he safely got me back to my apartment. He wanted to walk me up the stairs to my door to say goodnight or, in this case, good morning. I didn't want him to fall, but he insisted, so together arm in arm we climbed the stairs.

He did give me a kiss which I wasn't expecting or wanting, and before saying goodbye he said he would be by later.

I didn't think later meant in a few more hours, but after I had finally fallen asleep, I heard a strong knock at my door. Hesitantly, getting up and walking to the door, I asked, "Who is it?"

"Susan, I'm Skip. Remember me? I met you at the cub tonight," he replied.

As I slowly opened the door, he said, "Is Paul here?"

"Gosh, no. He left around 0200. Do you think he could have had an accident? He definitely had too much to drink," I said. I was starting to feel a little worried, while not wanting to look directly into Skip's face and wondering how he knew where I lived.

"Yes, he definitely was too drunk. I'll keep looking for him. I have had to go looking for him many times before, and it always turned out not to be a big concern. Sorry to have bothered you at this hour of the night. Thanks, Susan," he said as we exchanged our goodbyes at my door.

I remember being shocked at seeing Skip's face when Paul introduced me to him at the club. He continued to play pool with other guys while I was there, so I didn't really talk to him. Paul told me he had been a gunner on one of the Heuy helicopters in Vietnam, and sadly enemy fire destroyed his lower jaw. His disfigurement was shocking! He expected to be at the hospital for two years while receiving bone transplants and skin grafts to his lower face.

Skip had two pedicle flaps from his neck attached to his lower mandible. This repair allowed for viable blood flowing tissue to be sutured to an injured area. This was an excellent way to graft good skin tissue to an area with little or no skin tissue, as in this case, for Skip. It required a long healing process and several surgeries. He seemed to be taking it as well as he could. I couldn't even imagine how he must have really felt.

Paul told me that at several parties they attended, Skip pulled out a picture of himself before the injury to show everyone. I happened to see that photograph one night, too. He had been very handsome. He was an avid car racer. I was told he was very competitive then and won lots of races. I wondered what his new life would be like now. I prayed for good results from the plastic surgery. I know if he had approached me walking on a sidewalk or worse, in an alleyway on a dark night, I would have been frightened to death! It took a lot of getting used to seeing his disfigurement. So sad.

I was reminded of Samuel Goldwyn's movie, "The Best Years of Our Lives" released in 1947 after WWII.[43] It was the story of three soldiers returning home after the war to a life that was now so different for them. Their families seemed like strangers. One member of the cast was not really an actor but a true soldier who lost his arms in that war. He used hooks for hands. His role in this film gave inspiration to other disfigured soldiers. The movie received eight Oscars with best picture being one of them. I had seen this movie several times and always cried!

Also, Skip's condition reminded me of a book I read shortly before entering the Army called "Johnny got his gun" written in 1938 by Dalton Trumbo. It was about the horrors of war and, thankfully, the compassion that followed. Several of us in the military talked about it at gatherings.

I wasn't looking forward to seeing Paul again. My tolerance of heavy drinking was slim, since living with an alcoholic father for several years. Too many sad situations were conjured up in my mind.

He did come by as promised that next afternoon, and this time he was sober. He seemed more willing to tell me about himself. So, after offering him a soda, I sat and listened.

"I grew up here in Denver, so I see my folks from time to time. I haven't been released from rehab yet, but it is getting close. As you see, I can get around pretty well on this leg now," he explained with a sense of pride.

---

[43] Robert E. Sherwood and MacKinlay Kantor, "The Best Years of Our Lives," (1946) movie

"I am glad. I was a little worried when you took me for a ride last night. I was afraid you might dump the bike over," I said hesitantly, not wanting to "pour salt in his wound."

"Oh, I wouldn't do that. My pride would have been hurt. I can't let that happen. Captains are to remain stoic at all times you know," he laughed.

He actually did seem pleasant now. We spent the rest of the afternoon getting to know each other better. When I told him I was also from Denver, we had to compare our high school experiences. He was surprised to learn that I was shy and not pretty or popular while attending high school. He didn't believe me. He told me he was class president in his senior year and had a girlfriend he planned to marry when he returned from Vietnam. But, when learning of his injury, she sent him a "dear John" letter. Honestly, I didn't think he was over it yet. He added that a lot of his friends just never came around to see him anymore when he became a patient here. I was feeling sad for him.

We had a few dates, and one afternoon when riding on his bike we passed the BOQ where he lived. Ken was just coming out of the building and our eyes met, so I waved.

"Oh, do you know each other?" Paul asked.

"Yes, we met several weeks ago. I introduced him to a girlfriend of mine. I haven't talked to either of them since to see how their date went," I replied.

"We don't like those West Pointers!"

"Who is "we" and why not? I asked sharply.

"Man, they think their shit don't smell!"

How crude I thought. What an answer. I knew now who had "class" and who didn't. He continued to tell me that coming out of West Point as Captains, they would get command of troops immediately on landing in Vietnam. He said they were not experienced, and often led their men into dangerous situations.

With a slight chuckle, he added, "Some of these guys get wounded but not from the enemy, if you get my drift."

I didn't want to keep company with Paul any longer. I was saddened for his medical condition, but his personality was not to my liking. It was time to say goodbye.

CHAPTER SEVENTEEN

One afternoon, coming home from work I saw Ken sitting on a bench in the quadrangle just outside my building entrance. I wasn't sure if he was aware that this was my building since I had never invited him to my place. But he didn't seem surprised to see me standing there in front of him. I had not gotten back with him or Nancy after they had their first date, so I was interested to hear how it went.

"Hi, Ken. Nice to see you again." I greeted him warmly while approaching him somewhat hesitantly.

He looked up with the sun's glare in his eyes. "Hi Susan, I was actually waiting for you."

"I don't remember telling you my address."

"Listen, the information the government has logged in our personnel records makes it easy to know everything we want to know about each other," he grinned.

"Wow! Okay. Come up to my place as it is too hot out here! Plus I promise I now have something in my kitchen besides just ketchup," I said laughing.

I noticed he had some difficulty going up the stairs. I had never asked him what type of injury he received in Vietnam. I probably could have asked Katie since she was well informed of all her patients' medical histories.

He didn't seem to struggle as he sat down on the sofa. He mentioned he liked the apartment and noted the spaciousness with the extra bedroom.

"It was designed for two to live here, but I feel lucky to have this apartment to myself," I replied, while standing in the kitchen preparing lemonade for him.

I still had that bowl of cookies (probably stale by now), so I offered him some.

As he reached for a cookie, while holding his drink in his other hand, he said, "Susan, I really appreciated you thinking of me when you introduced me to your friend Nancy. We did go out, if she hasn't already told you, but I haven't asked her again."

"Oh, I am sorry to hear that. I thought you would really hit it off," I replied regretfully. I sat down in the chair next to the window across from the sofa.

"My interest is in you, not anyone else. That's why I came to see you today. I thought you enjoyed the evening we had together, so I was taken by surprise when you suggested I meet your friend. I am curious, so I must ask. Was it because of my limp?" he asked, while staring out the window behind me.

I sensed he was afraid of what I might say.

"No, not at all. I have not asked what happened to you, but as a nurse, I promise I can deal with anything. Really. It was the cowboy boots!" I smiled, while asking if he needed any more lemonade.

He started to laugh, "What?"

"Even though I lived on farms and even a large ranch when I was young, I am not into the cowboy/cowgirl thing. Don't get me wrong. I like western music, but it's not my favorite. However, Hank Williams' song "Your Cheatin' Heart" was one of his I liked to sing from time to time. Plus, he and I have the same birthdate! So he must be a great guy!" I added with a wink to uplift the conversation.

"Would you consider going out with me again? I want another try at this relationship, if you are not with that guy you were talking to on the phone when I first saw you."

Taking a deep breath, I answered, "No, I broke up with him. I didn't tell you this, but he also has a corvette. Maybe I am attracted to guys who drive sport cars," trying to smile, while holding back a few tears.

Continuing, I said, "I think he cared more about that car of his than he cared about me. So I decided it was fruitless to continue to beg him to come out to see me."

"I'm sorry. I didn't think the conversation was going well when I accidently overheard some of it."

"That's okay. I guess it just wasn't meant to be. And, yes, we can have another date," I sighed, while finishing my drink of lemonade.

Surprising to me, our date was at a Sunday church service. I thought about Katie and her patients sitting in the front pew near the pulpit. I never inquired about this unusual date; I just enjoyed the sermon as I always did and having him there with me seemed to satisfy our spiritual needs at the time.

Ken was an intense person to the degree that it sometimes made me feel uncomfortable. I knew he was quite intelligent, obviously, since he had been a West Point graduate with a ranking near the top of his class. He had periods of depression that I wasn't sure how to deal with, even with my psychological training as a nurse.

I remember one day he was sitting on the lawn outside the BOQ reading a book. I slowly approached him. He greeted me warmly, as I think he appreciated the company. He confided in me his periods of extreme sadness and depression. I believe he considered suicide at one point. I was surprised and saddened that this war could destroy lives either literally or mentally.

He was extremely ambitious and wanted to be a foreign diplomate. He was fluent in one or two other languages in preparation for that role.

He met my family and, not only did my parents and brother, Gary, really like him, but my favorite aunt as well. She was staying at the house for a week to help with mom when we stopped by one afternoon. She was a farmer's wife, and she thought I should marry someone like Ken. I think mom was just relieved he was not a Catholic.

Ken didn't seem to let his injury interfere with his interest in sports. He was quite strong. He didn't have the musculature of Pete, but at times he complained of cramping in his upper thigh muscles after some of his strenuous workouts. He enjoyed snow skiing and water skiing. I had not been in a pool since my introduction to Brad during basic training, so my fear remained. I never went with Ken on these outings; I assumed they were part of his physical therapy.

I think part of his depression stemmed from the fact that he wanted to make a career of the military after graduation. He was infatuated with the life of General Patton, which I am sure many West Point cadets were since Patton was also a West Point graduate.[44] He had an amazing military career, and Ken wanted to emulate him. So sadly, having to be medically discharged from the Army was heartbreaking for him.

A movie had been released in 1970 on the life of Patton, staring George C. Scott.[45] I didn't ask Ken if he had seen this movie, which won seven Academy Awards, but I imagine he had. I wondered if his injury occurred before or after that film came to the movie theaters. If I had used my psychological training more effectively, I would have pursued that question.

Fortunately, he was able to heal externally and internally. He had great determination, as well as ambition, as he planned a new career path for himself. I was glad of that.

My evenings and days off were usually spent with him. We enjoyed discussing lots of topics. It reminds me now of the movie, "My Dinner with Andre," where two old friends meet in a restaurant. For the one hour and fifty-minute-long film, the setting didn't change. I loved that! They simply sat behind a rounded corner table talking about their lives. It was a comedy, whereas our conversations were much more serious. When we

---

44   Wikipedia, "George S. Patton," https://en.wikipedia.org/w/index.php?title=Goerge_S._Patton&oldid=1020880367
45   Wikipedia, "Patton (film)," https://en.wikipedia.org/wiki/Patton_(film)

discussed his future life dreams, I knew the life he wanted wasn't the kind of life I wanted.

I was afraid I would be shoved into the background and not find my own identity. I would always be known as Ken's wife and not for anything else. I remember telling him I didn't want to become like Joan Kennedy, who became an alcoholic while living life as a senator's wife. Tragic really. Even glamorous and famous Elizabeth Taylor had a wonderful acting career, but after marrying Senator Warren, her life became so different. She spent most of her time alone on his farm. She began to drink more and more from what I read. I think that is why the marriage didn't last. She said, "He was married to the Senate." If Ken entered into the political arena with his current and future associations, this might have been my fate.

He said a few times I was a complex person and hard to read sometimes. That surprised me, but he was not the first one to tell me that. I knew nursing was an important career for me, and I knew I would never have children, so marriage didn't seem to fit into my plans. Because he wanted all of that, I broke off our relationship after a few months to the dismay of my family and possibly him as well. I still missed Pete, and I didn't feel it was fair to invite someone else into my life until I felt ready, and then only if their views on children and marriage matched mine.

Ken wrote me a beautiful letter to win me back not long after his medical discharge. I didn't hear from him again until three or four years later after he completed his PhD. His dream career was unfolding for him, which he wanted to share with me. It was the day before I married Pete.

"How unfortunate for him," Cyndi sighed. "Remember what I said about blueprints? It wasn't meant to be," I replied.

CHAPTER EIGHTEEN

It seemed strange to often see Ken's corvette parked near the curb of the BOQ when I crossed the street to go to work. I sometimes wondered what he was doing, but I never made any attempt to see him again. Nor did I ask Katie about his healing progress.

Work kept me busy. I was assigned to the plastic surgery service. My responsibility included scrubbing on their cases, cleaning the instruments, and ordering new instruments and other specialty equipment required for their surgeries. The instrument packs and surgical packs (linens) had to be set up the day before the scheduled cases. These packs were then autoclaved for sterilization. Since the plastic surgeons were allowed only two operating days, I scrubbed or circulated on other cases the remaining days of my schedule.

I really enjoyed working with the corpsmen assigned with me. Some were so funny and entertaining, while others expanded my mind. As I said before, many of the corpsmen were smarter than their superior officers, some having multiple and/or advanced degrees. I felt happy for them that they were stateside and not stationed in Vietnam. One corpsman would sit along the wall near the door of one of the suites each morning in a lotus position with his eyes closed. I worried sometimes that I would startle him out of a trance. He said he never slept at night, and this meditation helped him. Quite an interesting young man. I loved hearing him talk about philosophy.

After arousing him to let him know it was time for us to set up for an ortho case, he opened his eyes and said, "'There will always be rocks in the road ahead of us. They will be stumbling blocks or steppingstones; it all depends on how you use them.' Nietzsche!"

"Wow! I am impressed! One of my first patients was a professor of philosophy at the university. He liked giving me quotes like that, too. I always wanted to take philosophy courses, but never had the time with all the other required classes," I sighed.

> *"The Will to Truth, which is to tempt us to many a hazardous enterprise, the famous Truthfulness of which all philosophers have hitherto spoken with respect, what questions has this Will to Truth not laid before us! What strange, perplexing, questionable questions! It is already a long story; yet it seems as if it were hardly commenced. Is it any wonder if we at last grow distrustful, lose patience, and turn impatiently away? That this Sphinx teaches us at last to ask questions ourselves? Who is it really that puts questions to us here? What really is this "Will to Truth" in us? In fact we made a long halt at the question as to the origin of this Will —until at last we came to an absolute standstill before a yet more fundamental question. We inquired about the value of the Will. Granted that we want the truth: why not rather untruth? And uncertainty? Even ignorance? The problem of the value of truth presented itself before us—or was it we who presented ourselves before the problem? Which of us is the Oedipus here? Which the Sphinx? It would seem to be a rendezvous of questions and notes of interrogation. And could it be believed that it at last seems to us as if the problem had never been propounded before, as if we were the first to discern it, get a sight of it, and risk raising it? For there is a risk in raising it, perhaps there is no greater risk." <u>Beyond Good and Evil</u> – Friedrich Nietzsche*[46]

---

46 Friedrich Nietzsche, translated by Helen Zimmern, "Beyond Good and Evil," Chapter I. Prejudices of Philosophers, page 4, paragraph 1.

I remember another corpsman told me, while we were setting up for an GYN (gynecology) case, that his roommate was interested in me.

"How can that be? Have we ever met?" I asked, while laying out the sterile instruments on the back table.

"No, not yet. I am working on that for both of you," he laughed as he wiped down the two large overhead lamps that were directed into the surgical field.

"Okay, since we have never met, where does this interest come from?"

"Well, first I told him your name. He liked the sound of that. Second, I told him how cute you are. He liked that even better. Third, I told him you really didn't care much for the Beatles, who seem to make most girls go crazy and that you preferred classical music. He was excited to hear that, too. Does that answer why I am working on getting you together?" he laughed.

"Very interesting," I answered.

"He is a great guy. He works in personnel records."

"Well, then I guess he knows more about me that I do," I laughed.

Continuing, the corpsman said, "He wants to know your mailbox number?"

"My mailbox number? Okay," I answered with suspicion.

He continued, "He told me he wants to send you a note as to when, where, and what time he could meet you. He will place it in your mailbox."

"Goodness, this is sounding intriguing! A bit of mystery. Okay, I'm game," I replied.

"Great! He will be excited when I tell him. He has been asking so many questions, since I mentioned a new nurse arrived that it is making me crazy! Maybe this rendezvous will finally put an end to that," he sighed.

CHAPTER NINETEEN

I looked for that special note in my mailbox each afternoon after getting off work. Fortunately, I didn't have far to go since the post office was in the lobby of the hospital. I don't know how many military personnel were stationed at this post, but I assumed each of us had a box as there were two large walls of them. Mine was located just a few inches above my shoulders, thank goodness.

After a week went by and no note appeared, I decided this was just some silly prank. But walking back to my apartment after getting off duty, I heard footsteps behind me. I walked a few more paces, and finally turned around to see if it was my imagination or if someone was following me. Indeed, a guy was following me. Immediately, I decided this must be that guy with the phantom note.

I didn't make any gestures towards him but kept on walking. Finally, he called out to me when I reached my apartment building.

"Hello there," he shouted.

As I turned to look his way, I asked, "Are you the guy with a note about the time, date and place that never showed up in my mailbox, or was that a mysterious misdirected code?"

"I guess you could imply the first. That code idea sounds good, however. Probably the timing gives me away," he sheepishly answered.

"Okay, so there was never going to be a note. You just hid around the corner behind one of those huge marble pillars in the lobby to see who came to that mailbox each day. Then if you liked what you saw, you would make your approach. Right?"

"Absolutely! You got it!" he grinned.

Smiling, I said, "Very cunning!"

"Before you go into your building, do you mind if we sit and chat awhile?" he asked hesitantly, as if a rejection might be forthcoming.

Right away I knew he was not my type because we were the same height! Silly maybe, but I liked wearing 2" to 3" heels when I dressed up for a nice evening event, and this would make me taller. Not good!

But I agreed to sit and talk awhile…..I mainly listened. He seemed quite loquacious, probably because he was nervous.

"My name is Joe. My mother is Czechoslovakian, and my dad is Italian. I look like my dad. I have an older sister, who is married to an Italian, and I have a smart sweet little five-year-old niece. I was president of student council in high school and have a college degree in political science. Okay, you probably think I will be going to law school after this gig is up. But you would be wrong, even though my dad wants me to become his law partner back home in Delaware. Instead, I am heading for California to get a master's degree in film production. I like jazz and classical music; I can sing, and I play the piano well. I don't have a girlfriend right now. I was born in March, and I am a year older than you. I looked up your birthdate in your file. By the way, you and my mother have the same birthdate! How cool is that? Any questions? Oh, I almost forgot…..I am a nice guy, and I can be very funny as well. I also like clowns and harlequins! Now, any questions?" he asked, looking my way instead of staring down at the pavement.

"That was a quick synopsis or perhaps resume, " I commented as I raised my eyebrows, while looking into his sad puppy brown eyes.

"I'm not looking to hire anyone right now," I grinned.

Continuing, I added, "That is cool that your mom and I have the same birthdate. We are Virgos. I like that! We are interesting people if I do say so myself. So, if we should become friends, I need to know if you and your mother get along well."

Appearing more relaxed, he said, "As a matter of fact, we have always gotten along great. She is my biggest fan. She has always been proud of me and my sister too. I guess you could say we are one small happy family."

"Now, tell me about yourself, if I don't already know the answer," he winked and smiled.

I did like his smile, and my intuitiveness told me he was really kind and I liked that. He didn't seem arrogant and was intelligent as well. I knew when I started dating that I liked guys who were smart and ambitious. I always wanted to learn from them.

"Curiously, what is in my personnel file?" I asked.

"Oh, I can't divulge that information. They just might cut off my head," he laughed.

"All right," I said as I continued. "This is my hometown, but I was born in Nebraska. My parents live a few miles from here. I have a brother in the Navy and another brother living at home for now. My older sister is married and left Colorado a few years ago. I'm a nurse as you already know. I don't like jazz, but I do like classical music. However, my favorite composer is Gershwin, and my favorite composition is 'Rhapsody in Blue'. I am afraid of clowns and hated going to the circus as a little child as those performers scared me. I am shy, an introvert. I hate being in crowds; I get claustrophobia easily. Actually, I have many phobias, but I won't mention all of them now. I like going to art museums. My favorite artists are Botticelli and Ingres. I wanted to be an artist when I grew up, but things changed. I love my current job, but I hate this war and I want it to end ASAP! I cry easily. I'm too emotional for my own good sometimes. I like to read biographies and the classics, not romance novels or mysteries. Someday when I have the time, I will read 'War and Peace.' There! Any questions?" I asked, taking in a deep breath.

"Yes, where did you get that sexy voice and that cute face?"

"Next question," I grinned, slightly embarrassed.

"Do you know where there is a nearby piano?" he quietly asked.

"Really? Yes, as a matter of fact, there is a baby grand in the day room across the street in the BOQ," I replied.

"You out rank me lieutenant. Do you think I can even enter the building without getting court-martialed?" he asked somewhat jokingly.

"I won't tell anyone you're a noncom. That will be our secret," I smiled with a wink.

We slowly walked across the street, and silly me, I made sure I was not too close since he was not very tall. I was also happy to see that Ken's car was not parked at the curb as I didn't want to run into him. I'm quite sure he never broke any rules and would report Joe being on the premises. Sounds sad, but there were lines of demarcation in the military. Fortunately, these rules were more relaxed on a medical post.

Once we entered the building, Joe quickly walked over to the piano and sat down. The place was incredibly quiet, so I was a little afraid if he started to play something, everyone might come out of their rooms to see what was going on in the day room.

I assumed I was going to get a recital, so I quietly sat down in a nearby chair. To my surprise and shock actually, he starts playing from memory Gershwin's "Rhapsody in Blue." Suddenly I got very emotional, hurrying to stand next to the piano to watch his fingers fly over the keyboard. Tears started to form, and I was a little embarrassed about being so emotional. After he finished I could hardly express my appreciation. He seemed pleased at my touching display of gratitude, and, in fact, I think he probably expected it.

There was no going back now. I felt this overwhelming connection with him because of one piece of music! Karma? Serendipity? From this point forward our friendship was set in stone.

CHAPTER TWENTY

With all the fun times I had with Joe, going to plays, musicals, museums, and dinner, I still missed Pete. I remember sitting in the tub one night, crying like a baby and watching my tears trickle into the water with a splash. I hoped the apartment walls were thick enough so the neighbors could not hear me, or they might call the MPs to investigate. I felt I had made a terrible mistake breaking off our relationship, even with distance being a big factor now.

Pete told me his parents liked me, so, I decided to call his mom since I had that phone number. It was probably easier to reach them since Pete didn't have a home phone, and I didn't want to bother him at work. Plus, I didn't want to make a scene over the phone should he not want to get back together.

I finally dried myself off and looking at the clock I felt it was not too late to call. When I heard the phone ringing on the other end, I almost hung up. I was nervous. Suddenly, I heard, "Hello."

"Hi, Mrs. Powell. I hope it isn't too late to be calling you. This is Susan," I stated with some trepidation.

"Oh hi, Susan. How are you?" she pleasantly asked.

"I'm fine, I said while quickly trying to think of a reasonable reply. The reason I am calling is that I noticed I have two of Pete's sweaters here. In the rush of packing I must have accidently put them in my suitcase. He probably doesn't need them right now since its late summer, but I thought he should know where they are in case he was looking for them. They are both very nice sweaters, and I know one is cashmere. Since Pete doesn't have a phone at his apartment, I decided to call you so you could let him know."

"Well thank you, Susan. That is so thoughtful. I'm sure Pete would prefer that you tell him yourself. Honestly, I think he really misses you. Phil and I were so saddened to learn that you had broken up. That is why I was so pleased to hear your voice after I picked up the phone. Today is Friday, I think. Why don't you give him a call tomorrow at work? He told us he had a display he was building, and he had to work on it tomorrow to have it finished by Monday."

"Thanks for that information, Betty. Yes, I have been sad as well. I really enjoyed meeting both of you in El Paso and taking that short trip across the border to Juarez to have lunch. I will call him tomorrow," I answered as we said our farewells.

I slept so much better that night, and I couldn't wait to call Pete the next day. I hoped his mother was right and that he did miss me. I would soon find out.

"Pete?"

"Susan! This is a nice surprise. How are you?" he asked.

Hearing his voice and the inference that he was pleased to hear from me made me happy.

I quickly replied, "I'm fine. I talked to your mom last evening to tell her I had two of your sweaters, and she said I should call you today. Did you know you were missing two sweaters?"

After describing them to him, I realized he was aware they were missing. He was always well dressed, and his clothes were color coordinated as well as being a bit expensive. He always wore climbing boots for casual outings and leather black or brown boots for special occasions. He didn't wear cowboy boots like Ken did, but rather Florsheim side zipper lower heel dress boots. Even his socks were cashmere. Also, he didn't believe in wearing ties. He hated how restrictive they were, so he always wore turtlenecks with his dress pants. I am sure he knew his biceps bulged through. Despite the fact he said he never worked out; he was proud of his physique.

These memories were suddenly rushing through my mind. We talked for an hour or so, and when he told me he really missed me, I felt he was being sincere. I got emotional and started to cry. He said he finally got new tires for his car and had extra money saved up so he could come out to see me if I would let him. I was so excited!

He arrived a week later to stay only for the weekend, but I was so happy even if it was for only two days! He did meet my mother, who by this time was not doing well at all. I don't think she remembered him coming into her room and talking to her at her bedside. Dad did not like his long hair and smooth uncalloused hands. Otherwise, I honestly don't remember what we did while he was with me, but the time went so fast. We were both sad when it was time for our goodbyes. Once again, it was reconfirmed in my mind that this relationship was meant to be.

CHAPTER TWENTY-ONE

Going to work Monday was difficult. I wanted that DD214 (discharge paper) in my hand. I arrived on time and found out I was assigned to an oral case for jaw reconstruction. I hated working on those cases. I decided I would never have that done, even though a few orthodontists said I had the worst malocclusion they had ever seen. This after having braces on my teeth for several years in my youth. I wasn't going to let an oral surgeon rearrange my mandible and maxilla and wire my teeth together for weeks if not months, while I sipped my meals through a straw.

I did have a dental procedure done at the request of a few of the Army dentists. They appreciated my cooperation and said my picture would appear in dental books. Of course, the photograph was only of my mouth, thank goodness. Many experimental procedures were performed on willing subjects. Innovation was going on throughout the major hospitals, especially during war time. Treatments for severe burns and skin grafting were quite successful during the Vietnam war. That impressed me!

I walked through the double swinging doors into the operating room, after the ten-minute betadine soap brush scrub waiting for the circulator to tie the back of my sterile gown and apply my face mask. At the same time I couldn't help thinking about the wonderful weekend I had had with Pete. I couldn't wait to begin my life with him.

"Susan, I hope you didn't have a swinging weekend. We have a long day ahead of us," the colonel said after he entered the room. He opened the linen pack and took out the hand towel to dry off his arms and hands before unfolding the sterile gown.

"I'm up to the task," I replied. I finished seeing that all the instruments were well placed on the back table. My mayo stand was positioned near me at the end of the operating table and organized the way I liked it for handing him the hemostats, sutures, and sponges.

Kellys, the largest straight and curved hemostat clamps were secure atop a rolled sterile hand towel, followed in line by the criles, a little smaller, and then the cute little misquitos. The different 0 to 6-0 silk and cat gut sutures were also lined up in order of size.

I was glad I didn't need the 10-0 nylon suture that ophthalmologists used on their cases. It was barely visible to the naked eye. The surgeons had headlights and magnifiers to help them see, not only the fine threads of suture, but the microscopic field where they were working.

I remember taking my exam, having to know the different suture types, the needles used whether tapered for going through soft tissue or cutting going through the skin. Suture used in the organs and surrounding tissues was cat gut, either plain or chromic and each dissolved at a different rate. I loved learning all these particulars and knowing the names of the different instruments used for each type of case. I remember almost laughing when setting up the instruments on the back table for an orthopedic surgery. They looked just like the tools dad stored in the garage.

The bovie cautery was ready with the electric cord clamped to the sterile drape covered around the patient's neck to prevent it from dropping down into contaminated territory, which was any space below the sterile field. If the bovie malfunctioned, that could have been a disaster. The area behind the throat was very vascular and surgeons, regardless of the case, needed to have bleeders (cut blood vessels) clamped and cauterized as soon as possible to avoid a bloody visual field. They needed to see the area they were working in without interference from too much blood pooling.

Saline wash was always ready for surgeries, as well as different suction tips applied to the hoses that extended from the vacuum machines which were mounted on the walls of the operating room.

The largest operating rooms were used for the biggest cases and usually for open heart surgeries. The open-heart bypass machine took up a lot of floor space. Often five to six surgeons were standing along the sides of the operating table, three to each side, while the scrub nurse stood near the end of the table.

I never liked this assignment, because the nurse was too far back from the operating field to adequately see what was being done at any time. So having the necessary tool or item available to place with a "snap" into the surgeon's hand was difficult to do. We could only rely on the verbal command. The anesthesiologist had the best view, standing at the head of the table while administering the anesthesia.

I recall one cardiac surgeon would come into the operating room with his hands shaking. They continued to shake throughout his cases. All of the staff felt very uncomfortable working with him, worrying that he might cut an artery, and the patient would exsanguinate or bleed to death. It wasn't long before he was shipped out to Vietnam. I hope he took better care of himself and his skills while there. He had a terrible drinking problem, of course, which caused the tremors. He probably had to have a drink before he got out of bed each morning. Unfortunately, I was told alcoholism was a big problem in the military.

I made sure to always wear my elastic stockings, knowing I might have to stand in one spot for hours at a time. Even then, by the end of the day, my legs ached. I also wore clogs. My "friend," the oral surgeon I was working with on this case, told me he always wore clogs. They were comfortable to slip into and out of while standing for long hours, especially in one spot. I followed his advice and always wore clogs for the rest of my nursing career.

I was glad he was cordial and greeted me without any hostility. I wasn't up to any deriding. Not today. He drove around the post on his days off in his white 911 Porsche convertible. No one else had a vehicle like this, so everyone knew it was him. I loved that car! When I mentioned how much I liked it during a case one day, he decided that was reason enough to ask me out. Sadly, he was married with his family living in another state. I liked his work, and he seemed nice enough, but when I scorned his advances, he was not happy.

I had heard of, and actually worked, with some very temperamental surgeons. I know a few would throw instruments across the room, hitting the operating room walls.....just out of frustration! Not a pleasant situation at all!

Please let this day pass quickly I thought to myself, as the long tedious case began.

"I had also heard of angry surgeons throwing instruments during a case. How terrible. I am glad I didn't work in the OR," Cyndi stated.

CHAPTER TWENTY-TWO

Sometimes when there was adequate staffing and we were done with our surgeries for the day, we would take over for someone if their case was continuing for several more hours. If nothing else, the scrub nurse needed a bathroom break and/or lunch. Unfortunately, the surgeons did not have this luxury. I remember only once seeing another surgeon step into the room, asking if he could relieve his cohort.

I recall after about four hours, slipping out of my clogs from time to time and stretching my back muscles, the sergeant, who I had that unfortunate experience with on the night shift, came in to tell me someone phoned from the lobby, asking to see me.

"Who is it; do you know?" I asked.

"He said he flew in this morning from California and had to talk to you. I believe he said his name was Charlie. That's all I know," he replied.

Suddenly, the surgeon said, "Aha! You have a beau!"

"He is not my beau!" I retorted.

"Well, that's sad. Like all the rest of us, he probably wishes he was your beau," the surgeon muffled under his mask.

Surprisingly, the sergeant interrupted, asking if I wanted to break scrub. He added that he would fill in for me until I returned. I was so glad he asked, not because I was eager to see Charlie, but because I needed a bathroom break!

"Sure! Thank you so much," I said, moving away from the operating room table. I was trying not to disturb any nearby implements while being thankful we were doing our best to be cordial to one another. Neither of us wanted anymore reprimands.

I had to remove my scrubs and put on my "civilian" clothes that I always wore to work before I could go down to the lobby. Because of the morning chill, I had worn my green suede coat along with my leather below the knee brown boots. I also wore a brown beret into work that morning, along with my brown and green plaid scarf for color coordination.

I loved to be stylish. When I was still in high school, I loved looking at the beautiful fashion designs in "Seventeen Magazine." I wanted to design clothes as a career back then as well as being one of the models on those pages. Cheryl Tiegs was my favorite! I wanted to emulate her. But I had the hair style of Twiggy, the famous English model of that time. I was glad I wore this outfit to work. I wanted to look my best, so Charlie could see what a terrible mistake him made with that "dear john" gesture. I guess I wanted to rub mud in his face!

As I was getting ready, I remembered a new nurse who was assigned to our department. I decided I had a little competition because she was quite beautiful, not that I really wanted any competition. She was 5'10" tall, with dark brown hair and blue eyes and carried herself like a model. She had just returned from her year-long tour of duty in Vietnam. Her name was Mindy Collins.

One day during a break from our cases, we started a conversation. When I asked her where she was stationed in Vietnam, she answered Da Nang.

"Oh, I had a fiancé who was stationed there," I replied.

"What was his name? I may have known him." was her response.

"Charlie McDaniel."

"Charlie! Yes, I knew Charlie. Wow! He was popular. Great guy and quite a looker, I might add. Gee, Susan, he never told us he was engaged!" she said looking pitifully in my direction.

I could only imagine what was going through her mind at that moment and surmised she was one of his many concubines.

Now, I was even more furious as I pressed the elevator button for the hospital lobby.

As the elevator door opened onto the first floor, there was Charlie wearing casual clothes and standing by a white marble pillar. He was one of the few lucky warrant officers who survived that ill fate in I-Core.

"Hi, Susan. Gee you look great!" he smiled.

"As do you," I replied, not wanting to appear excited to see him.

"Thanks for coming down. I wasn't sure when I called if you could get time off to see me," he continued.

"I can't be away long. I still have a long case waiting for me," not wanting to encourage a lengthy conversation.

He continued, "I'm staying at the Hilton near here. I fly home the day after tomorrow, but I flew in here hoping we could get back together, Susan. I have really missed you. I still love you; you know."

"Oh stop! How can you even say that! What happened to all those other girls you became intimate friends with over in Vietnam?"

"What makes you think I even dated anyone over there anyway? Aren't you making preconceived assumptions?" as he looked at me sternly trying to dissuade me.

"Does the name Mindy Collins ring any bells?"

I knew immediately by his expression that I hit a nerve!

"How do you know Mindy Collins?

Almost ready to scream, but remembering we were sitting in the lobby of the hospital, I softly said while smiling, "She works here in our OR."

"She does?"

With some hesitation, he continued, "Yes, I met her in Da Nang when I was there. Nice person I recall."

"Well, she had a lot to say about you!"

I added, "Charlie, do you really believe we can have any kind of relationship, considering everything that has happened since you gave me that engagement ring? It is ridiculous!"

"Wait a minute. I came all the way from California to see you. That should mean something. I'm out of the military now, and I want us to make plans for a beautiful future together," he explained.

"No, Charlie. It is too late! I am glad to see you are okay. Did you receive any battle wounds? Do you have a purple heart?" not really waiting for an answer.

"By the way, where are my modeling photographs that you insisted you needed to keep me close to your heart? Also, did you paint my name on your Huey helicopter as you promised? Of course not, you forgot my name as soon as you landed on Vietnam soil!"

"Have a heart, Susan! Gee!"

"Anyway, Charlie, I am with someone else now. Remember Pete? He came to our apartment party when Mary and I first moved to El Paso."

After a slight pause, I continued, "I let him read your letter saying I should go out and have a good time instead of waiting patiently for a year like a good little girl while you were gone. He told me then you were playing around. It didn't take you any time at all, did it?"

I think by this time, Charlie was justified in assuming we couldn't continue where we left off. This relationship was probably doomed from the start for reasons I wrote about earlier.

Cordially, we said our goodbyes as the elevator door opened to take me back upstairs.

CHAPTER TWENTY-THREE

I think I finally realized the reason dad and mom didn't want me enlisting into the military when I arrived at Fitzsimmons. They didn't want me to get hurt. I could say I was naïve, as I mentioned previously, and my actions proved that numerous times during this two-year tour of duty.

I don't know how many surgery interns were assigned to this hospital, but I believe with all honesty they wanted to have a liaison with me, regardless of whether they were married or not. This reaffirmed my disillusionment with the sacred vows of matrimony.

One intern asked that I take care of his two beautiful dogs while he and his wife were away on a two-week R & R (rest and recovery). I loved animals, and after he invited me to his house to meet them and his wife, I fell in love with his slender long-haired year-old dogs. I thought his wife was quite nice, a bit plain, but a nice match for him. Just prior to their departure, he was on call and asked me to come up to his call room for instructions he had forgotten to mention earlier. I was uncomfortable, but I had accepted the assignment to feed, exercise, and groom the dogs, so I went to his room. Nothing happened because, fortunately, I sat in a nearby chair, listening to his instructions while he was lying on the bed. After knocking, and entering the room, I made sure to leave the door open. About ten minutes after I arrived, a group of surgeons stopped by, seeing the door was ajar and looked in to say a word about the case schedule for the next day. I felt embarrassed seeing them all look in at me. I knew immediately what they were thinking as they greeted me and smiled at the intern. I was happy at this point to say I had to get back to my apartment as I had all the instructions I needed.

Another intern, who worked on a few ophthalmology cases with me, asked me out for a picnic. I decided to accept, since I was not with Pete at the time. It was summer and beautiful in the mountains. We enjoyed talking about our childhood experiences when we had a few minutes between cases, so I decided this would be a fun day off. Everything was going well; he brought the lunch, the blanket and even some wine. Our dessert consisted of passionate kisses followed by wonderful sex. Maybe this was his intent all along, but with him I didn't seem to mind. I welcomed his embrace and gentle touch.

I felt such tranquility when we were together. No pretenses. I truly enjoyed his company, as he did mine. We rested for a while, listening to the sounds of the forest while gazing at the beautiful blue sky. The singing birds, the chipmunks scurrying along the forest ground, and the soft rustling of the aspen leaves from the gentle breeze rounded out the ambience.

After a few hours we noticed clouds appearing overhead, some being nimbus clouds. Suddenly, I felt a drop of rain on my forehead. It was time to gather the food basket and blanket and walk back to the car. Neither of us wanted this special moment to end. But the blissfulness ended abruptly when he turned to me and said he had something to divulge. Oh no! Here it comes!

"Susan, I loved this afternoon. This was wonderful, even magical! But I don't want to mislead you going forward. I have been married for two years now," he said, while softly caressing my hair and gazing into my eyes.

Not uttering a word, I looked away.

"I am so sorry. I don't love my wife; it was an arranged marriage. Our parents belong to the same country club, and after she came out as a debutante, my parents decided she was the one for me. We don't have similar interests, and we don't seem to want to spend time together. I felt some relief at joining the Army just to get away. I found you to be intelligent and attractive, and I liked being with you. I wish I had met you two years ago, then my life would have been perfect," he continued as tears appeared in his eyes.

Not sure how to respond, I turned to face him, and taking his head into my hands, I told him, "Thanks for a beautiful day. I too will always remember this time I had with you."

After we wiped away more tears mixed with a few rain drops, we packed up and drove back to Denver. We didn't exchange many words, but I sat close to him in the car, while he had his arm around my shoulder. It was going to be difficult to work alongside him on future cases. But, que sera, sera!

One morning while I was sitting alone in the colonel's office after my OR case had just ended, he stopped at the door to tell me he was leaving the next day to return home.

Solemnly, he said, "I wish I could stay. Thanks for being a good friend and listening to my family troubles. I will really miss you, Susan. I know you don't want to hear this, but I do love you and will keep the picture of you in my wallet forever. I hope you will do the same with my picture. Not to sound cliche, but thanks for the memories."

We didn't try to approach each other. We both felt guarded and needed this space or barrier between us. I smiled and told him I would also keep his picture in my wallet. I didn't tell him I loved him, but I did think we would have been happy forever if God had meant that for us. From time to time I would take his photo out and think of the "what if."

CHAPTER TWENTY-FOUR

I remember on one occasion I had to attend an event that required my wearing the military blue uniform issued to me during basic training. I actually liked this uniform. I don't remember if I attended the event alone or went with another nursing friend. But I do remember after entering the dining area that I focused on a long table with people seemingly enjoying their meal and conversations. Immediately, I saw the intern and his wife who asked me to take care of their two dogs while they were away. My instinct was to walk over and say hello. Regrettably, I noticed when his eyes met mine, he quickly glanced away. There was much laughter at the table, and on further inspection I realized these interns had their wives with them. Several of the other physicians looked my way and let me know with their stares that I was not to come near them. Suddenly, I felt cheap! I wish now I had remained that ugly duckling. I wanted my fairy god mother to change me back, or better yet, let me just disappear!

A few other liaisons occurred, some too uncomfortable to even mention. I had a lot of learning to do that came with Army enlistment. Being a female in the military seemed to signal to the male sex that it was open season, and anything was game. Sometimes it was difficult to hold my head high!

I didn't become a nurse because I wanted to marry a doctor, as was the intent of many other nurses. Also I didn't join the Army to have an affair with one of the other officers. I truly wanted to help the hurt and wounded, no matter their lot in life and no matter where I worked. This was the pledge I made to God. There were times I felt I was another Florence Nightingale trying to save the dying from their emotional, physical, and sexual infirmities. Deep down in my heart I knew I was a hard-working caring person. I was a good nurse! But at times an attractive female living the Army life made that conviction more difficult to pursue.

"Oh, that is so sad!" Cyndi replied, while giving me a hug after we had finished our lunch.

CHAPTER TWENTY-FIVE

On my special ETS (expiration – term of service) date, I was so happy! Pete, as promised, picked me up at the Army Post after I signed out and received my final pay in cash. I had never seen or held so much money at one time in my hand. I don't remember if I said goodbye to anyone, but I'm sure I must have. I do remember I was asked if I wanted the $10,000 bonus to reenlist for another tour of duty. I didn't hesitate to say, "no thank you!"

Even though I was proud of my chosen profession, I wanted to erase the sad and difficult encounters I had as an Army nurse and move on with my life with Pete. I wanted to get into another field of nursing where I could actually see and talk to the patients, as I did before I enlisted in the military. Rainbows were now beginning to emerge at the end of the horizon.

By this time, my mother had passed away, and my father was married again. This angered me! I am sure he was having a relationship with this new woman while my mother was still alive. I remember meeting her once or twice after they married. They lived in her home while my brother, Gary, lived by himself in our house. I guess they were deciding which one to sell.

Pete drove us to my home in Denver in my 1971 convertible Volkswagen. He told me he was proud of my car selection, even though his interest was in corvettes and Porsches. He especially liked the blue color (my birthstone sapphire) with the grey convertible top. We were going to spend some time sightseeing in Denver before driving to Illinois.

Our plans were abruptly interrupted, however, after that first night. My father stormed through the front door early in the morning while Pete and I were still sleeping.

As we rushed to get dressed and go into the living room to greet him, we were met with the following words!

"You are no longer a daughter of mine! Get out now! I came here, finding you sleeping with this man! You should be ashamed! You are going against God's law! I forbid it in my house!!" he yelled.

Puritan ideology was prevalent during the fifties and sixties. If someone didn't go to church every Sunday, they were looked upon with some disdain.

I remember as a young child walking in on a conversation my mother and two of her sisters were having, while sitting at our kitchen table drinking coffee one afternoon. My mom, leading the conversation, voiced her consternation of an appalling obscene situation linked to some young girl in our small town and how it was an embarrassment to her parents and their friends. The rumor was that they planned to send her away to live with a distant relative. I didn't fully understand what I was hearing, of course, but allegedly, this girl had become pregnant out of wedlock. When my mother noticed I was accidently eaves dropping on their conversation, she chastised me and told me this conversation was for adults only, and I needed to leave the room. Sex before marital vows was forbidden!

Interestingly, during the eighteenth century and continuing into the twentieth century, the term Grundyism or simply "Mrs. Grundy" was referenced with matters relating to sex or nudity by moralistic or straight-laced individuals. Mrs. Grundy was a figurative name for an extremely priggish person. She was an unseen character in the 1798 comedy play by the Englishman Thomas Morton called "Speed The Plough."[47]

---

[47] Wikipedia, "Thomas Morton (playwright)," https://en.wikipedia.org/w/index.php?title=Thomas_Morton_(playwright)&oldid=1012922528

By the early 1970's, the encroachment of the European hippie movement into the United States was defined as deciding life was about finding oneself and rejecting the need to conform to the mores of the times. The constraints on the definition of sexual morality were eased.[48] I don't say that I condone or affirm these new moral changes, but that was the era I lived in then.

After dad's ranting, Pete tried to reason with him, but sadly it didn't work. Actually, I had never seen my dad that angry. He didn't stay around to make sure we had left, but we were out the door within the hour. I didn't even have time to take any of my belongings, other than what I had brought from my apartment at the Post. I couldn't even say goodbye to our family dog, Prince. He was out and about that morning making his rounds. My brother, Gary, had been taking care of him after the rest of us had left home.

I later learned that Gary had called my dad to make him aware of my sleeping arrangements with Pete. He also disproved. About a year later Gary sent me some of my most cherished belongings. I think he finally felt some guilt and sadness about my sudden departure. He and I had been so close as brother and sister before I entered the military. We confided in each other so many times. How sad this ended so abruptly.

I remember we were with my mother when she passed away on a sunny October Saturday afternoon. I called our pastor to come and pray with mom. Gary and I gave each other comfort and strength to deal with this sad experience. Dad was not home, and we didn't know how to contact him. So mom died with only Gary, me, and our Pastor at her bedside. When dad returned several hours after her body had been removed, I screamed at him, using a few expletives to emphasize my disapproval of his absence. I don't remember if he replied to my harsh criticism. He slowly walked over to sit on the living room sofa while keeping

---

48 Yeoman Lowbrow, "The Decade of Decadence: A Quick Look at The Sexual Revolution." March 2, 1015.

his back to me. As he stared out the window, I am sure tears flowed. His feeling of guilt had to be unsurmountable. I do know he stopped drinking after her death.

As often happens in family situations, when there is strife within the family structure, that strife is brought to the forefront, especially when one is dying. This occurred with me and mom. I mentioned that we did not get along well, so I confronted her on her death bed a few weeks earlier.

"Why did you not love me, mom?" I asked somewhat hesitantly.

Expressing no remorse she immediately replied, "Because you did not want my love."

I was shocked at this sudden statement. What child does not want the love of their parents? But I needed to ask her this question to have some understanding and closure.

I remember a few months earlier hearing her say to dad, "Don't let Susan have the piano when I'm gone!"

I didn't understand where this hatred came from. Sadly, I decided if I really wanted a piano, I would just buy one in the future. Which I did.

As for my dad, he did not speak to me for three years after I moved away, and then only at the request and probably pleading of his new wife. It must have been hard for her as it was for me, to understand how he could just erase me from his memory.

I did see my dad again. He moved to New York with a third wife. Through the years I tried to be with him on his birthdays as often as I could, especially since I lived closer than my brothers and sister, and they couldn't visit him as often. Ironically, since his second and third marriage didn't seem to last, I suggested that he live with his fourth wife before they married to see if they were compatible. He welcomed my suggestion and did just that! That marriage ended badly with his wife taking much of his furniture and cherished belongings, some of which were heirlooms from Denmark!

I remember once when I was riding in the car with Dad while heading to one of his farms, the topic of dying came up in the conversation. I told him, "We come into this world alone and we leave this world alone." I don't know what made me say that, and he didn't comment.

Dad passed away on a cold snowy January day in a New York hospital without any of his children at his bedside. I wanted to be there with him, but Pete wouldn't let me go due to inclement weather, both on the coast and at home.

CHAPTER TWENTY-SIX

The drive to Illinois was a two-day journey, and Pete didn't want to spend the money on a hotel. So we slept in my Volkswagen that first night along the side of a dirt road near some farmer's field. I was disgusted with his "thriftiness" but too tired from that restless night that I didn't express my thoughts to him. Getting to his place couldn't come soon enough. I was sad with my sudden departure from home and tired for lack of rest. I just wanted to lie down and sleep for as long as my body needed.

I had been to Pete's apartment a few times before. In fact, I remember one time flying out to see him for a long four-day weekend. I had worked the night shift and just packed up my clothes and left for the airport that Friday morning. I knew I could sleep on the plane. The arrival in Chicago was around 10:00 P.M.. I waited and waited, but no sign of Pete to pick me up at the airport! I noticed the last of the scheduled arrivals had come in while the terminal was becoming vacant. I sat alone near the entrance with my suitcase by my side, trying to decide if I should get a flight back to Denver that next morning or continue waiting for Pete to arrive.

"May I help you?" asked a young man who was passing by on his way toward the large sliding exit doors.

"Thanks, I am waiting for my boyfriend to pick me up," I said somewhat embarrassed.

"Have you been waiting long?" he inquired.

"What time is it now? I think I have been here almost two hours," I answered with some alarm.

"The terminal will be closing soon. I work as an airplane mechanic for TWA, and I am getting ready to go home. Can I drive you somewhere for the night?" he asked showing concern.

"Thanks. That is nice of you to offer. I tried to call my boyfriend at work since he doesn't have a phone at home, but there was no answer," as I sighed and took a deep breath.

"Wow! Do you know where he lives? I could drive you to his place," he continued.

"I remember some street names near his apartment. Would that help? If I see landmarks, I can point them out to you, too," I answered with some hesitation.

"Sure, I can do that for you. I know this area well," he assured me.

By this time, I was so angry with Pete. How could he do this to me? I wasn't sure if I could ever forgive him.

We drove through the cloudy chilly night around 1:00 A.M. until arriving at the streets that I remembered. Fortunately, I saw familiar buildings along the way. Eventually, we did arrive at Pete's apartment complex, and I instructed my driver to park near Pete's apartment door. I went up the steps and knocked – no answer. I knocked again and still no answer. I didn't see any lights on anywhere and didn't see his new red corvette. So he was either gone, or it was parked in his locked garage.

Exasperated, I told this helpful young man, Ed, to drive me to a hotel near the airport so I could get a flight back to Denver the next day. He did and helped me with my luggage after I registered. He then came to the room with me, which I didn't want him to do, but he seemed so kind and helpful. However, I had to ask him to leave when I realized he wanted to spend the night with me. Darn! Why should everything be so thorny!

After pleasant goodbyes, I decided to call Pete one more time at his place of work to see if he might be there waiting for my call. Sure enough, he was doing just that.

"Oh Susan, I am so sorry! I have been trying to get this design project done before the final deadline, and I fell asleep a few hours before your arrival time and didn't hear the alarm clock go off. Where are you now?" he asked regrettably.

For numerous reasons, I was exhausted, so I told him to pick me up in the morning. Again, I didn't express my discontent at his irresponsibility. After we arrived finally at his place, he was nice enough to fix breakfast for me while I unpacked a few of my things. I had forgotten from my previous few visits that he had sheets hanging from the windows instead of drapes or curtains. There was no bed frame, just a full-size mattress lying on the floor in his room. It seemed awkward getting up and down from the floor. The sheets on the mattress matched the sheets (light green with a geometric design) hanging on the windows. When I asked him if he was going to buy any curtains, this was his reply.

"Why should I? I have never liked window curtains or drapes. I like this modern design and color of the fabric. So, the answer is no," he emphatically replied.

Speaking as a designer, I was surprised by his answer. From the other furniture he had in his living room, it was quite evident that he didn't intend to spend any money on beauty or even comfort, at least for the time being. The sofa looked like he had picked it up from the side of the road after someone had discarded it. The springs were sprung, and the dark brown velvety covering was well worn and faded in places. His old TV set was given to him by his parents, I believe. It did work, but he seldom watched any programs or shows. He preferred to listen to rock music on his nice stereo equipment that he purchased at the PX (post exchange) while still in the military. The price of everything was much less than in retail stores. Bargains abounded! He and other military recruits took full advantage of this opportunity. Unfortunately, I didn't.

His second bedroom was set up for his work assignments. In contrast to the rest of his apartment, he had a beautiful large drawing board that appeared to be quite expensive. Lying on the tilted board was his current project. Ink drawings of the exterior of an apartment complex covered several large sheets of drawing paper. Each of three sheets showed the buildings from different angles. He explained this was an ad creation for a large construction company. He drew specific species of trees and shrubs in the foreground that he felt matched the exterior design of the buildings. It was beautiful to look at, and the precision was excellent! He was quite proud of his work, as was I.

The room had a bookshelf full of his art books from school and other books relating to art that he loved. Frank Lloyd Wright, the great American architect, was a great inspiration to him.[49] He had two books of his architecture. He was eager to show me pictures of the house and building designs as well as the interior furnishings created by Wright. He loved the contemporary lines. He said he wanted to see "Falling Water" built from 1935 – 1937, probably Wright's most-admired work located in southwestern Pennsylvania. It was a home cantilevered over a waterfall. He also wanted to see the Guggenheim Museum constructed from 1956 – 1959 in New York City. Thinking back, I believe Pete would have been better suited as an architect rather than an industrial designer.

Another book he showed me was "The Bauhaus School of Design." Bauhaus was a school of architecture, design and applied arts that existed in Germany from 1919 – 1933. It was founded by the architect, Walter Gropius, who combined two schools: the Weimar Academy of Arts and the Weimar School of Arts and Crafts. He called it Bauhaus, or "house of building." Students were trained in art and craftsmanship. Gropius' idea was that designs should be functional as well as aesthetically pleasing.[50] Pete loved this idea, and he frequently referenced this book. I heard the phrase "form follows function" often.

49 Edgar Kaufman, "Frank Lloyd Wright American architect," book published June 1st, 1955.
50 Editors of Encyclopaedia Britannica, "Bauhaus, German school of design," https://www.britannica.com>topic>Bauhaus

I had much to learn from and about Pete, so I decided to settle into this somewhat uncomfortable abode and decide about my future plans and career. My past life would probably become a distant memory.

CHAPTER TWENTY-SEVEN

I needed to find a job as I didn't want to depend on Pete for too long, especially financially. However, a situation came up that interrupted my plans for work. I think my mother was probably right. She didn't like me because she decided I was too promiscuous! I didn't see it that way; I just went along with the sexual times. The conversation she had with her sisters probably came into her mind several times in regard to my waywardness.

Unfortunately, I was a "baby boomer" born after WWII. We had reached our sexual prime by the early 1970's. We were no longer living in an environment of sexual inhibition. The more puritan aspects of previous decades were fading. The sexual revolution was considered by many to be the most shocking social trend in the 1970's. Surveys taken during that time reported that by age nineteen, four-fifths of all males and two-thirds of all females had had sex. Fashion designers promoted a new sensuality, producing miniskirts, hot pants, halter tops, and formfitting clothes designed to accentuate women's sexuality.

Two popular books of the era were "The Sensuous Man" first published in 1971,[51] which was basically an instruction manual on male sexuality. The other was "The Joy of Sex," which sold eight million copies since its first publication in 1972.[52]

I am not apologizing for being a young adult during that sexual revolution, but I didn't conform to the strict morals of my parents' generation. What my mother deemed as undesirable behavior seemed commonplace to my generation. We felt protected with "the pill" and other contraceptive devices. Abortions were now

---
51   Joan (Terry) Garrity, "The Sensuous Man," https://en.wikipedia.org>wiki>TheSensuousMan
52   Dr, Alex Comfort, "The Joy of Sex," first published 1972.

legal in some states because of Roe vs. Wade. By early 1973, Hawaii, Alaska, New York, and Washington state had legalized abortion laws.

In 1973 the U.S. Supreme Court ruled that the Constitution of the United States protects a pregnant woman's liberty to choose to have an abortion without excessive government restriction. It struck down many U.S. federal and state abortion laws and prompted an ongoing national debate in the United States about whether and to what extent abortion should be legal, who should decide the legality of abortion, what methods the Supreme Court should use in constitutional adjudication, and what the role of religious and moral views in the political sphere should be. Roe vs. Wade reshaped American politics, dividing much of the United States into abortion rights and anti-abortion movements, while activating grassroots movements on both sides. The Supreme Court issued a 7-2 decision ruling that the Due Process Clause of the Fourteenth Amendment to the U.S. Constitution provides a "right to privacy" that protects a pregnant woman's right to choose whether or not to have an abortion[53].

Unfortunately, this dilemma was now facing me. I didn't take the "pill," and I hadn't used any precautions during sexual intercourse. I didn't think I was promiscuous, but when I thought I loved someone, sexual activity became the endpoint.... not marriage and then consummation. I actually thought I must have been sterile because of my lack of preparedness, while sexually active during those few years when I didn't get pregnant. But that had all changed now.

I stated previously that I never wanted to have children, and Pete expressed that as well. He was interested in his art, and I wanted a career in nursing. But when confronted with this decision, I was torn.

I remember one evening a few years later, a physician, who was a patient of mine, asked, "When do you believe life begins?"

---

53   Wikipedia, "Roe v. Wade" https://en.wikipedia.org>wiki>Roe_v._wade

I was taken back by his question, but I answered as honestly as I could, "I believe life begins with the soul. If the soul is present at conception, then that is when live begins. If the soul becomes present at birth, then that is when live begins."

If I had contemplated this question in 1973 when I realized I was pregnant, I may have made a different choice. Today, I regret my actions back then. I believed I would never have children, but it never crossed my mind that it would be by choice this way. I loved Pete, and he was quite forceful in his decision that I have an abortion. So off to New York City we went.

CHAPTER TWENTY-EIGHT

Sitting next to Pete in the taxicab driving through the crowded streets of New York City on an early gloomy and cloudy, chilly morning, I remained silent while Pete talked with the driver. At one point, I remember we drove through the Bowery! This was the skid row area of the city with vagrants, alcoholics, and drug addicts meandering about. I was shocked to see so many lying on the sidewalks either asleep or passed out with no protection from the weather. There was a lot of trash along the curbs of the streets, blocking the storm drains. Trash containers were overflowing! What a sad mess! I couldn't get this image out of my mind. But, I had other concerns facing me.

After arriving at our destination, we slowly walked up the several steps to an old brick building. Once inside, I was directed to a waiting room, while Pete was guided into another part of the building. There were maybe twenty young girls close to my age sitting in the chairs and sofas in that large room. As I looked at their faces, I could feel their sadness and remorse, as I am sure they could also see from my expression. The staff members were very polite and informative. I was given a sedative. Then I was directed into a small dressing room to change into a hospital gown and given disposable slippers to wear as well as a paper hat. I was also given a number written on a small piece of paper. That number would be called when it was time for me to be escorted into the treatment or surgical area. This anonymity gave each of us some comfort. I recall none of us initiated a conversation with anyone sitting nearby. The stillness was eerie.

The physician was kind as was the attending nurse. He explained the procedure, and fortunately, I was able to recover quickly. My naiveté of this entire ordeal probably aided in my maintaining some sanity. But as the weeks and years passed, I felt regret and sadness.

My Christian upbringing made me feel ashamed! I didn't want anyone to know of this act of mine. But sadly, I remember confiding in my brother, Gary, several years later, after I thought we had reconciled our relationship.

"You will go to hell. You know that don't you?" he affirmed!

Our relationship lost ground once again.

I wanted Pete to have a vasectomy. But he refused! He didn't want any scars on his body! I recall he was even proud that his sperm could travel so far as to get me pregnant. What gall! He didn't show any sensitivity to my emotional state. After an evening spent with his younger brother and his wife who had just had a baby girl, I went home and cried and cried.

"What in the world are you crying about?" he asked, lacking any cognizance of what I had just been through.

This insensitivity on his part should have been a "red flag" for me. Several times I was told by his friends that he was a "man's man." I wasn't really sure what that meant, but his inattentiveness to my needs probably fit into that mold somewhere.

After a few weeks of healing physically and mentally, I decided to apply for a job at some of the local hospitals. I needed to focus on something else. After two years in the military, I felt that emptiness or loneliness, as I was suddenly being integrated into "civilian life." I remember a few times I drove through the gates of the nearby military post just to feel that sense of belonging again. I missed that military camaraderie. One afternoon I even parked the car and walked up the steps to the officer's club front door. I wanted to go inside and join those officers sitting at the bar, even though I didn't really enjoy drinking. But I knew military life was not available to me now. Maybe I should have accepted the Army's invitation to send me to medical school.

The Veterans Administration Hospital offered no positions in the OR (operating room) since a Monday through Friday day job was too attractive for many nurses. But I didn't want to work in the OR anymore anyway. In fact, I was told there were no openings for nurses in the hospital and there was a waiting list of fifteen nurses wanting to apply for jobs. The benefits were excellent! But because I had just left the military, the Chief Nurse said they would make a position for me. I felt grateful and was offered a nursing position on the Kidney Transplant Unit. I wanted to take care of veterans, especially since I was a proud member of that group. Plus I could now see them and give hands-on-care, unlike working in the OR when the patients were sedated and lying under sterile drapes. Maybe I could begin to see a different rainbow.

CHAPTER TWENTY-NINE

I was excited to go down a different nursing career path. I was sure I would love my new role on this twenty-one-bed unit, taking care of kidney transplant patients. But I never wanted to care for children or women after my experiences as a student nurse, working in labor and delivery and also working on a pediatric ward. Instead, I wanted to take care of the male veteran population.

Sadly, I remember, having to start IV (intravenous) fluids after puncturing the tiny veins located on babies' heads so medications could be administered. The image of them crying and screaming from the ordeal, even after applying a topical anesthetic, will never leave my memory. Also, seeing young children with maladies or ill health lying in those hospital beds brought tears to my eyes. Some of them were suffering from the terrible diagnosis of cancer. I thought how unfair that some of these young children might die before they even had a chance to live their lives!

But to my surprise, there were small children and women on this unit. Under CHAMPVA (Civilian Health and Medical Program of the Department of Veterans Affairs), a surviving spouse or child of a Veteran with disabilities, or a service member who died in the line of duty was eligible for health care services and supplies.

The first patient who greeted me after I arrived on Monday morning for 7:30 orientation was a cute little five-year-old boy! He came walking down the hallway towards me to say hello, while carrying a little stuffed brown bear under his arm. We smiled and introduced ourselves, as I knelt down to greet him. He was in the hospital to have a liver transplant.

Quickly I had to learn a new set of skills that were not required in the OR. Initially, I was assigned to work the night shift, and each morning I had to draw ten or more tubes of blood from the newly transplanted patients. The values were then written on a large flow sheet located on the wall outside the patients' rooms. When the surgeons came for their morning rounds, these numbers showing kidney and liver functions were available for their review.

Transplant rejection was a large concern. When the body recognized the new organ as being foreign, this tissue could be rejected by the patient's immune system. So the renal or kidney lab results were the most revealing in showing if rejection was taking place. The patients couldn't wait to see what the lab values revealed. We felt badly for the patients if their lab numbers were going in the wrong direction. That meant possible removal of the organ, and if it was a kidney, then dialysis had to resume.

The patients had arteriovenous (AV) shunts or fistulas which were used for dialysis. A procedure was performed to connect an artery and a vein. In the early seventies, this shunt was visible on the exterior of a patient's arm. If those vessels were too worn out, then the shunts were placed in a lower extremity. A technique was used to attach each vessel via the shunt tubing to an artificial machine, which would perform the function of the kidney by filtering and removing waste products.

It could take up to six months to determine if the new organ would be accepted, so patients usually had lengthy hospital stays. Fortunately, their rooms could be decorated with mementos from home. They had family photos, posters, as well as furniture and other colorful décor decorating their rooms. Sometimes the patients could go home for the weekends while wearing masks to avoid getting infections. But, because of their long hospital stays, the medical staff became their extended family.

I also had to start daily IV (intravenous) infusions to administer some of the ordered medications. The term "pincushion" was used often among the patients and staff. We hated to have to puncture their skin with needles every day and usually more than once. They had bruises on their arms which took a few months to completely disappear.

I loved working on this unit and caring for the patients' physical and emotional needs. More than half were women. I stayed on the transplant unit for four years. Throughout my forty-one-year nursing career, this was the most rewarding experience.

CHAPTER THIRTY

One night after I had tape recorded my report to be heard by the day shift staff, one of our renal fellows entered the office as I was putting things away. His name was Frank. After finishing his internship and residency, he elected to complete a fellowship in nephrology. He was a kidney doctor. I was somewhat taken by surprise and a little nervous on seeing him standing in the doorway.

One morning the previous week, I gave a verbal report to the oncoming day shift nurses. With my back to the door entrance, I sat in a chair facing the other nurses, and mentioned that I didn't like this new fellow's bedside manner. I didn't think he showed enough rapport for the patients. The Head Nurse kept trying to signal me that he was standing behind me at the time. Unfortunately, it was too late when I abruptly stopped talking about his demeanor. He actually smiled when I turned to look up at him, but no words were exchanged between us.

So, on seeing him in the doorway several days later, I decided he wanted to confront me about my allegation now that we were alone. Interestingly he didn't even bring that subject up. He started off with a very different comment.

"I think I know you," he calmly stated.

"Oh, I doubt that really," I replied.

Looking at my name tag, he continued, "I never forget a name."

Believing he had me confused with someone else, I continued, "I just recently moved here. I am actually from Colorado."

"I know," he replied.

"You know?" I asked with alarm!

"Yes, I actually know a lot about you," he answered with great confidence!

I suddenly became speechless. So he went on to say, "I received my undergraduate degree from the University of Colorado, but I was raised in New Mexico. Have you heard of "The Manhattan Project?" Before you answer, I will just tell you that my father was hired to come to the states from Germany to help with the nuclear bomb. Something I am not proud of, but he was a nuclear physicist," he said while looking downward towards to floor.

"Wow, an intense time for you growing up, I imagine," I answered while trying to think of a more pleasant topic.

"Since you went to CU, would you have possibly known John Speck? I dated him a few times," I answered.

"Oh really? I knew John well. I remember he also went to medical school. Smart talented guy! I dated his sister, a few times," he smiled.

Continuing, he remarked, "But that is not why I know you. Do you remember someone in your life named Jeff Banks?"

"Oh my! Yes! We dated for a while before I joined the Army two years ago. How do you know Jeff?" I asked with surprise showing all over my face.

"Well, Jeff became my best friend while we were stationed together in Italy. He talked about you all the time. He said you were an extraordinary girl! He was sorry things didn't work out between you. He said you told him you became engaged shortly after entering basic training. But I see from your name tag, you still have your surname. I guess you changed your mind then?" he queried with his eyebrows slightly raised.

Not wanting to explain my intentions regarding that engagement, I simply answered, " Yes. Sadly, I did get engaged to a young man I met during that time. But you are right. It didn't work out."

Suddenly, realizing that I was having this conversation miles from my home in Colorado with someone who knew Jeff was almost shocking! It truly was a small world! I didn't ask if he was still in contact with Jeff. The day crew would be arriving soon, and I was tried from working the night shift, so we said our goodbyes.

After I married Pete, I saw Frank again only once. He saw me sitting at a desk in the nursing station of the CCU (Coronary Care Unit) one morning. He was asked for a consultation about a kidney problem on one of our patients, so he stopped to say hello. I learned a few years later he and his wife divorced. Someone remarked that she was mean to him, which made me sad as he seemed like such a nice guy. He spoke fluent German, and after his divorce, he left America. Later I was told from some of Frank's colleagues that he had an IQ of close to 200. No wonder he knew who I was after reading my name tag, and that he remembered so many details reported to him by Jeff.

CHAPTER THIRTY-ONE

I felt Pete and I were settling into our living arrangement. It was not my intention to move in with him, had dad not rushed me away from home. After first securing a job, I wanted to have my own apartment. But, unfortunately, that would not have been possible anyway.

Pete would ride his bicycle to work as often as he could, not only to save money for gas, but also to protect his corvette. Washing and waxing that car became a weekly ritual. We shared in the cooking and paying for our living expenses.

Pete got along well with the apartment manager/owner, and soon we moved from a second story apartment to a ground level apartment with the garage entrance door off the kitchen. Pete preferred this to having to go outside and down a flight of stairs to the garage at his first apartment.

Early one afternoon about three months into our life together, Pete came home early, a day that I had off. I was surprised to see him walk through the front door. He said he had been fired!

"What? You say you have been fired?" I asked with such surprise.

"Terry decided I was in competition with him, and he forced me out. It is that simple," Pete answered, showing no physical emotion.

"How sad. With your talent I can't imagine the business letting you go like that," expressing my disbelief.

"Rita said she didn't want to let me go, but because Terry had been with the company several years, she decided to act on his request. She said she was sorry," Pete answered.

The next day Pete worked on his portfolio and planned to get interviews with other design companies around the state as well as neighboring states. I was sure he would find a new position very soon. But to my surprise, the biggest design businesses turned him down. I was shocked! Why? I wondered.

I started to worry about this since I knew Pete could be very forceful. He had a commanding presence and had the utmost confidence in himself. Even his stature could be somewhat imposing. After meeting him and going out a few times, I pictured him at the top of Maslow's hierarchy of self-actualization. I had never met anyone with such drive and determination to succeed.

Maslow's hierarchy of needs was proposed by Abraham Maslow, an American, in a paper he wrote in 1943 called "The Theory of Human Motivation" which was published in *Psychological Review*[54]. These needs were presented in a triangle with physiological needs at the bottom of the pyramid. Safety needs next, followed by love and belonging, then esteem, while self-actualization was at the top. His belief was that we as humans started at the bottom of the tier and worked our way up after the needs of each tier were met. We needed air, water, food, shelter, sleep, clothing, and reproduction before we could move up the ladder to safety needs, such as personal security, employment, resources, health, and property. Friendship, intimacy, family, and sense of connection was next on the tier. Respect, self-esteem, status, recognition, strength, and freedom came after that. And desire to become the most that one can was at the very top. Very few ever reached that top rung, I recalled from my reading. So, I was impressed and intrigued that Pete, to my mind, actually did reach that acme.

I don't remember how long it took him to find another job, but I decided not to worry too much about it. We had some savings, and we were able to pay all the bills on time. I wanted

---

54 Wikipedia, "Maslow's hierarchy of needs," https://en.wikipedia.org>wiki>maslow's_hierarchy_of_needs

to concentrate on my new nursing career. Plus, I decided to go back to school. I did not have that four-year nursing degree since I went through a three-year diploma nursing program. I couldn't afford the tuition for the five-year program offered at the University of Colorado, and I felt that was too much time out of my life. I felt confident with my training, as all of us took the same state nursing boards for our licensure anyway. Plus, I noticed while working as an aide one summer at a local hospital, between school years, that the RN I was assigned to work with on the night shift did not know as much as I did about care for the patients. Her knowledge base was limited, I thought, even though she had just graduated from the university program.

However, some inferiority came over me when I was in the Army. The four-year nursing graduates received their silver bar when they entered the service, while those of us with the three-year education came in with the gold bar. We were second lieutenants, and they were first lieutenants. My observation of many of them when we were assigned to set up mash units during basic training caused me to notice they lacked many skills that I had learned with much OJT (on the job training). I thought it slightly unfair that they outranked me, so I decided then I needed that degree.

CHAPTER THIRTY-TWO

Pete found employment with another designer. There were no other employees, and they worked out of an old railroad car located in a field outside the city. Three-foot-tall grasses almost obscured a third of the train car from front to back, but the entrance was always cleared of wild growing shrubs. It was actually a nice place for inspiration, I thought. Very quiet, but not ideal for welcoming customers. Definitely not what I was imagining for Pete's career, but he was satisfied, and they seemed to have a lot of business.

I enjoyed my classes at the university, while continuing to work on the Kidney Transplant Unit.

The transplant unit was originally located in a park-like setting on many acres of beautifully wooded land. I believe there was a stream flowing through the property as well. This provided solitude and tranquility for the patients if they wanted to stroll the grounds. Originally, the land may have been purchased by the Veterans Administration for housing mentally ill patients. This was the perfect environment for them. I admired the large, beautiful stately homes lining the left side of this street as I drove to work each day and hoped to someday live in a home such as these.

Sadly, after driving through the iron gates at this location for three years, administrators decided to move the unit to the main hospital about five miles away. This was temporary as the new chief of the Nephrology Unit, a surgeon just out of the Navy, wanted to move the unit permanently to the university hospital after remodeling was completed.

What a change! The neurology ward had to accommodate us until the final move could be arranged. All the nursing staff felt somewhat cramped as we tried not to get in each other's way. Since I wouldn't have a job soon on this abandoning unit, I decided to transfer to the Coronary Care Unit (CCU) or heart unit a few months later.

We had had a few renal patients come into our transplant unit with very high potassium levels, and consequently, they almost died. We had to take acute resuscitation measures to help them survive. Sadly, some of these patients deliberately tried to raise their blood potassium levels because they didn't want to live any longer. I wanted to get a better understanding of heart related illnesses by working in the CCU.

Before that transfer occurred, I was making my rounds, checking on the patients after my night shift started. I heard a whimper coming from one of the rooms. Slowly I pushed open the door and lying on the bed curled up into a fetal position with her back towards the door was one of our favorite patients.

Cindy was a very pretty 21-year-old, four years younger than me. She had been on dialysis after losing her kidney function from a condition called eclampsia which she developed during pregnancy. She fit the criteria with her young age as she was nineteen when she became pregnant. She was from a very poor family, so her nutrition was probably not adequate; and this was her first pregnancy. She developed hypertension, or high blood pressure. Unfortunately, as often happens with this diagnosis, she lost her baby. She did not have a supportive husband or understanding family regarding her current medical status. She was placed on home dialysis after her kidneys failed. Her husband was immature and having him as her partner in setting up the dialysis machine was difficult and probably daunting for both of them. The medical staff learned after she had a kidney transplant and went through a painful divorce that her husband had a drinking problem. One day he took a gun and shot bullets into the machine, alarming and frightening to the ears of all of us, not to mention what it must have done to Cindy!

Her parents were divorced when she was very young, and she had no brothers or sisters. Her mother didn't write or visit as I recall. Her body had rejected one new kidney, and this second donor kidney was not functioning as anticipated. Sad outcome. She was going to have to resume dialysis again. She had already had several external shunts from previous dialysis treatments, and a new one was recently placed in her right lower leg for the anticipation of this second kidney rejection and resumption of dialysis. Sadly, she had many scars on her upper arms and abdomen from all the required surgeries. She remained quite thin, and her skin tone was ashen. She abandoned her daily grooming and no longer put a brush or comb through her long blond hair. Her depression was worsening!

I softly called out her name as I approached her bed. She slowly turned to look up at me, while wiping away tears trailing down her cheeks.

With a weak, soft voice, she said, "Susan, I can't do this anymore. I don't want to live like this. I am so tired!"

"Oh Cindy!" I replied as I walked closer to her bed.

"See that full moon shining through my window right now? I just stared and stared into that bright light and decided to pray to God. I told him I didn't want to remain on this earth. I want Him to take me home now. I know I am supposed to dialyze this morning, so I am going to tell Dr. Evans I'm going to refuse," she peacefully continued.

I sat down beside her and gave her a big hug. "You understand what this means by not doing the dialysis?" I returned with tears now falling down my cheeks.

"Yes, Susan. I have thought about this for quite a while now, and I am fine with this decision. I believe God is accepting of this, too," she replied.

I put my arms around her shoulders and squeezed her tightly, while trying to comfort her. "This is between you and God, and I certainly will accept your choice. This morning I will let the staff know about your decision. We truly love you Cindy! You have been through so much in these past few years," I answered, hoping I was providing some solace.

When I gave the night report to the day shift nursing staff, the neurology employees were also present in the report room. There were gasps and cries coming from almost everyone when I told of Cindy's decision. The renal fellow was pouring a cup of coffee at the time, and as he turned to hear my words, he almost dropped his cup.

"I will go see her immediately," he said.

I quickly followed him down the hall as he headed towards her room. I wanted to be there when he tried to convince her to change her mind.

After quickly greeting Cindy, he seated himself in the chair in the corner of her small room facing her bed. He explained all the ramifications of her decision not to have further dialysis. I stood close to the door looking at his expression while he spoke. Then I turned to look at her, waiting for her answer. She appeared tired and probably didn't sleep much that night, especially since we had our discussion from 1:00 to 2:00 A.M. that morning.

She reaffirmed her undaunting decision. Surprisingly to me, he began to shed tears. I was pleased to see this emotional response from him, as so often physicians, especially surgeons, are quite stoic. Their mannerisms or body language, when talking with patients about dire outcomes, are usually difficult to discern.

I had two days off after this night. When I returned on the third day, I was told Cindy had passed away early that morning. Her suffering was now over. I wish I had been at her bedside when God took her away.

CHAPTER THIRTY-THREE

The 12-to-8-night shift was rough on my body. I was assigned this shift probably every two weeks. Since it messed up my biorhythms, it usually took two days of interrupted sleep before I felt fully recovered.

I remember at the start of one of my five-night shift schedules, I dragged myself off to work while Pete was sound asleep. After parking in the employee lot, I walked into the hospital first floor corridor and stood in front of the four main elevators, waiting for one of them to open and take me to the sixth floor.

As usual, at this time of the night the hallways were quite dark. Spooky really! A lone security guard was sitting near this secondary entrance which gave me some sense of safety. There were two small lamps mounted on the wall across from the elevators that gave almost candle-like illumination. Occasionally, while waiting for one of the elevator doors to open, I would be greeted by another employee, usually a nurse or aide who was also waiting to start this shift.

Tonight, however, I didn't see anyone I recognized. Instead, interestingly there were two men leaning up against the far wall, both wearing trench coats, as this particular night it was raining. Just one more "Alfred Hitchcock" or "Stephen King" eeriness to add to this creepy scene. I tried not to look their way and kept my head down, hoping the elevator door would hurry up and open.

Once I was in the elevator I knew I would feel safe. But as I entered, one of these two men also entered. Oh dear! It was just the two of us in this small cage of an elevator. I didn't acknowledge his presence as I pushed the button for the sixth floor and hoped he would be getting off before I did.

"Hello. Do you recognize me?" came a deep low voice from this strange man.

As I slowly raised my head to focus on his eyes and face, I didn't think I knew him. I wondered who would be asking me such a question at this time of night, especially since he was apparently not an employee of the hospital. He had a mustache, a long beard, and from what I could detect under his hat, a head of long dark brown hair.

"I'm sorry, but I don't think I have ever met you before," I answered with some uneasiness.

"I'm Joe!" he declared, knowing that the elevator was fast approaching the sixth floor.

"Joe?" I astonishingly asked.

"Yes! I know my appearance has changed drastically since I last saw you. But don't you recognize me from my "sad puppy brown eyes" that you said you loved?" he questioned with a grin.

With total dismay I replied, "Joe! My goodness, I can't believe it! You are here? How did you find me? How did you know I was in this state, and how did you know I would be working tonight in this city and at this hospital?"

"Notice this Sherlock Holmes coat I am wearing? Well, I am a sleuth!" he grinned as he pulled out a pipe from his coat pocket.

Glancing at my watch, I sadly replied, "I have to be on duty in a few minutes; I have so many questions for you, but I don't think we have time for that here.

"Oh, my plan is to stay here until you get off work in the morning. I want to take you to breakfast. Then I can answer all your questions," he stated.

I knew that wouldn't work. Even though I didn't think Pete was the jealous type, I didn't want to upset him, so I declined the breakfast invitation. Joe did follow me down the hall when I finished my early night rounds. Fortunately, no one was stirring about, and all the patients seemed to be asleep. The nursing staff for the neurology patients were sitting in the lounge, waiting for patient call bells to ring.

We stood together looking out the windows at the end of the hallway. It was still overcast, but the rain had finally stopped. The moon was a hazy gray, slightly round image hiding behind the clouds. I pointed out to him my little blue VW parked in the lot.

"How did you arrive here? Did you drive or fly all the way from Delaware?" I curiously inquired.

"Oh! You remember where I'm from. Good! Do you also remember I was planning on going to California to get a film degree after that life interruption or military confinement?" he asked.

"Yes, I do remember you mentioning that," I replied.

"Well, I did go to California, and I did try to get that degree in film, but I stunk at it! So, I told "Fargo" it was time to go back home. Out of respect for my father, I will attend law school, and then decide if I should go into practice with him," he answered.

"Who is Fargo?"

He quickly turned to look at me and said, "You don't know Fargo? Well, he happens to be the best get-around-town and now the country of any vehicle I have ever owned. He is my best pal, my jeep! Heck, he met you when we were in Denver. Gosh, I can't believe you don't remember him. He told me he really liked you!"

We laughed. It seemed as if time stood still. It had been over three years since I had last seen him. He sent me a letter after being transferred to Hawaii for his last tour of duty before discharge. The envelope was thick, and I assumed the letter was lengthy. Joe had a gift for creative writing, and he could be quite loquacious at times. Unfortunately, looking back I wish I had read that letter. Instead I threw it away, unopened!

CHAPTER THIRTY-FOUR

Because I declined the breakfast invitation, Joe decided to stay over another day, and arranged to meet me after class the next evening. I found him sitting on a stone bench outside the science building. Students passed by him as they walked to and from class. He seemed to be an aberration sitting there, especially since he had that long somewhat straggly head of dark brown hair, full beard, and moustache. He could have been a homeless guy, which actually happened to many of the young men who came back after this war. But with Joe, these young students probably thought he was a professor sitting there mulling over his next class lecture before entering the building.

We took a long walk around the campus grounds as we discussed how we had spent the past three years of our lives. His goal in persistently pursuing me was to ask me to go back to Delaware with him. His firmest desire, I thought, was that we should be married and have a family. He was angry when I told him I had not read his last letter before he left for Hawaii.

"You threw it away without even opening it? Susan, I put my heart and soul into that letter. How disdainful of you! Do you realize that if you had read it, I probably wouldn't be here right now asking, or begging you to come home with me," he remarked with great angst and frustration!

Not wanting me to see his angry side for too long, and not wanting either of us to cry, he suddenly transformed into Marcel Marceau, the mime clown. With pantomime hand gesturing he urgently wanted to change this tragedy scene into a comedy scene. This was effective, even without the clown facial paint. He made both of us laugh. But, as with all clowns, the pain and hurt were still hidden behind that unpainted mask.

We reminisced about our military days. I think he even purchased tickets for an outdoor play that evening, but I don't recall the name of the play or even the theme. I think I was too nervous spending this much time away from Pete, even though I did tell him a friend I knew from the Army was driving through on his way home and wanted to see me before he left.

Pete didn't seem to be bothered in the least, as far as I could surmise. He said we didn't have the piece of paper that said I belonged to him. Of course, he was referring to a marriage license. Marriage had not entered into any conversation for Pete and me. I was taking the pill, so pregnancy was a distant concern now and I enjoyed my nursing career and taking these classes for my degree. I explained to Joe that moving to Delaware with him was not what I wanted in my life. We hugged each other and said our goodbyes. I wondered then if he would again pop-up somewhere in the future.

CHAPTER THIRTY-FIVE

My family was almost a distant memory for me now with dad's rebuke and my brother's scolding. My brother, Jim, and sister, Cynthia, were living their own lives in different states, but I knew someday we would arrange to see one another.

Dad did start calling me after three long years of silence, but only at the request and pleading from his wife, I believe. He soon learned of Pete's intellect and ability through our conversations, and that pleased him. He also came to visit with his third wife, as they traveled from Colorado to their new residence in New York. Having built a home for my brother, Jim, after he married, dad was impressed with the solid construction of this 8000 sq. ft. building that Pete was working on.

Pete had worked with his design partner for two years, until the business went under. He said Keith, the owner, was not a good businessman, and he allowed the business to fail. So Pete wanted to start his own business.

He spent a few months looking for property with the right zoning, and he wanted us to live on that property as well. He had previously experienced a few break-ins, either at work or at our apartment. Because of this, he wanted to protect his "tools" of business. Doing so required guarding them 24 hours a day which, of course, to Pete meant that we had to live at the same location.

He found the perfect piece of property outside the city limits. It was twelve acres with lots of tall, beautiful trees, as well as two streams running through the southern and northern borders. He said his spiritual connection to God came through trees. He was a "tree hugger." His childhood dream was to build a large structure, using his own design from his inspirations of Frank Lloyd Wright's buildings, which was not a surprise to me.

When we purchased the land, we were living in a duplex that was across town from where Pete and I initially lived. After the one-year lease was up, he wanted us to move into the part of the new building he had somewhat completed. It was the lean-to that would eventually be attached to the main structure. He didn't like paying rent and also paying for a property a few miles away. So, the best solution for Pete was that we cease paying rent and live in this small space. He said it would only be for six months until he could get the second story of the main structure completed for our living quarters.

I was reluctant and apprehensive about this move. I had just ended my job as the head nurse of a neurosurgical ward, a job he encouraged me to take when it was offered by the chief nurse of the hospital. But after two years he wanted me to resign, because I was spending too much time at work - usually twelve hours. He said he would divorce me if I didn't, because he decided my "life" was at the hospital. In retrospect, it actually was. The hospital became my sanctuary after tolerating living with Pete for so many years.

I always believed we were meant to be together, as I mentioned before. But life was extremely difficult. Forty years later after he passed away, many friends wondered how I survived.

"Gosh! I haven't met the right person yet, but if your life was so difficult, I hope and pray I meet the right one," Cyndi said with the voice of concern.

CHAPTER THIRTY-SIX

I remember a phone call from my dad addressing my unofficial marital status, "Why aren't you married? How long has it been now; a few years? Susan, he is using you! You are living in sin! Either get that license or get out!"

I pondered this for several weeks before I broached the subject with Pete. He was reluctant at first. But sadly, with three days of pleading, he relented and decided we could get married. He parents, as well as my father, were pleased.

He made a firm decision that we would go to the City Hall and get the license from the Justice of the Peace. Our witnesses would be employees there. I wasn't too happy about this, but I didn't see myself walking down a church aisle either. I was too shy for that. Also at his insistence, we had to go there on his motorcycle! He thought that was a splendid idea! So with our helmets and casual attire, we married his way and finally had that license!

When we arrived back at our apartment, one of his friends, who I liked as well, was standing on the step of our front door. He was surprised to learn we had just gotten married. When we greeted him, Pete decided for some reason, still unknown to me to this day, to slap me across the cheek! I was shocked and embarrassed, especially since Jerry was a witness to this indignation. And I was confused. What did I do wrong? I knew Jerry was embarrassed as well, and probably wished he could quickly disappear. I didn't say anything, but in silence my tears started to form.

What was wrong with him? Why would he do such a thing, especially on the day we finally became a married couple? I don't remember if I asked him why. But, if I did, I am sure in his mind he had a sound reason to chastise me. This was a red flag moment, and I did think maybe I should have left him on that day. But that thought passed.

I repeatedly tried to convince myself I truly loved him, and believed he loved me in his unusual way. Had I not left home the way I did and moved to an unfamiliar city where I had no friends, this matter wouldn't have confronted me. But here I felt some isolation and fear. I managed to make acquaintances with some of the other nurses I worked with, but these were only casual. After moving into the lean-to living space, which was not more than 600 sq. ft., I felt embarrassed to invite any friends to come over. And over time I learned that Pete didn't want me to have any friends. We could visit his friends at their homes, but I couldn't spend time with my friends. This life I was entering into was not what I expected after first meeting Pete.

CHAPTER THIRTY-SEVEN

Now I can admit years later, I wondered how I survived. If I had made any kind of misstep, I am certain I would not have lived through those years with him.

Pete had a love of guns and was an excellent marksman. For several years he went target practicing with a friend of his on Saturdays until his friend passed away. He was proud of his bullseye targets that he brought home to show me. I complimented him on his skill.

I was raised with guns in the family home. Living in the Midwest and on a farm, it was a necessary household item. I remember my dad had a loaded shotgun mounted above the fireplace mantle when we were living on the farm. If coyotes, or wolves, came into the barnyard during the night or early morning hours to find a delicious meal, dad would grab that gun and fire shots into the air to scare them away. Or if need be, kill them. Even though our chickens were in a coop, they were easy prey. Our young calves and baby lambs were also targets for the hungry scavengers. These farm animals put "food on the table," i.e. money in the bank for ranch owners and farmers. Their existence needed to be guarded.

But the love of owning guns and target practicing for skill was foreign to me. I had to learn to shoot when I was in the military, and I guess I passed that test. But I was not comfortable having loaded guns in the home, if it was not for the purpose I mentioned above. When Pete would leave home for an outing with his friends, not to return until late at night, he would always show me where a gun was, in case there was a trespasser or worse an intruder. This was especially concerning since our property was wooded and located outside the city limits.

When he began his design for the building, a fortress came to his mind. One could maybe describe him as paranoid, but he wanted to make the structure was as safe from intruders as possible. So I never really felt unsafe whenever I was alone on the property. My fear came when I upset Pete to the point of anger. Then I actually feared for my life!

"Oh dear, Mrs. Farwell. I guess you feel fortunate to have lived a long life then," Cyndi stated, showing distress.
I continued on with my story.

CHAPTER THIRTY-EIGHT

Woefully, living in this small area called "home" lasted for 35 years. Pete continued to work on the building, and I helped some for about 25 of those years. But after the passing of his mother, he lost interest. A housing development was going up across the road, which also upset him. Up to the point where he stopped, anyone who drove up to our place, whether a business customer or one of his friends, was in awe of his accomplishment, especially after learning he did all the work himself. The craftsmanship was startling, and this beautifully designed building complimented its park-like setting. Frank Lloyd Wright would have been proud!

A well and septic system had been installed before he prepared the ground for the foundation. So, fortunately, we had running water, but I never had a kitchen. I had a microwave oven and a two-burner hot plate for cooking. He rigged up a water line to come underground from the well through the side wall. An attached water hose was used for our drinking water and for filling our "bathtub", which, shockingly, was an animal trough. It was located in the corner near the wood stove that we used for heat during the long cold winters. A heating element was inserted into the tub to warm the water. There were no walls dividing one area of this small room from another. Everything was in the open. He built a full size two-bunk bed from extra construction lumber. It was very sturdy and heavy. He decided I was to sleep on the upper bunk while he took the lower bunk. He did build wooden shelves around the area of the hot plate and microwave, so I had space for a few pots and pans and any dishes and utensils I needed for cooking.

I was honestly amazed that I was able to create lots of delicious meals in this tiny space. He often told me I cooked like his mother. He liked that, and I was pleased he appreciated my meals. I worked the evening shift after we made this move, and I made sure he had a tasty hot meal each evening while I was away.

There was only one chair that he always sat in located near the doorway leading into the room. I had to sit at the end of the wooden bed where he built a small eight-inch extension. Years later I noticed I had developed scars from sitting on that rough wooden surface, even though many times I placed a towel or small pillow under me.

This lean-to, which was eventually to become a three-car garage, was temporarily divided into two compartments. We lived in one third of the space while our red 911 Porsche Targa convertible, purchased the year we were married, was parked in the larger room. This room also had some furniture, including an upright piano and an organ given to us by a friend of his. Eventually, all the furniture pieces were to be placed in the upper floor living quarters after it was completed.

Roofing shingles weren't going to be laid until the whole building was finished. So temporarily, Pete rolled out a rubber material for roof covering on the lean-to. He became frustrated over time as the frequent rainstorms caused leaking from the roof top into this building.

I remember trying to sleep on the top bunk while water dripped from the roof onto the mattress I was lying on. So I had to place small bowls all around me to collect the water drops, while I tried to remain motionless. Many times I cried myself to sleep. Pete didn't suffer that experience since he was on the lower bunk, and he slept soundly, unless there was a severe thunderstorm. Then surprisingly, he stayed up all night sitting in his chair and watching the radar screen on our rabbit ear TV, since tornadoes were prevalent in this part of the country where we lived.

When Pete started his own business, it was located on the apartment complex grounds, just south of our first apartment. As I said earlier, he and the manager/owner became good friends, so a cement block building was erected for his business. The other tenants were jealous and upset, so they tried to take revenge at times. After a tornado swept through the complex and almost completely destroyed this block building, Pete decided we should move to a duplex he found on the other side of town. He managed to salvage his tools, but he knew he had to find a new business location, so he was excited when he finally found this property outside the city.

CHAPTER THIRTY-NINE

The hospital was my refuge. As I mentioned before, I left that head nurse position at Pete's request. I decided to work the evening shift because Pete was a night owl, and I wanted to sleep when he did. I knew different sleeping hours in that small room would not work well for either of us.

The intensive care required of the patients kept me so busy that I didn't have time to think about Pete or worry about our marriage. I was excited to be working again in the CCU/MICU (coronary care – medical intensive care unit) and I loved the adrenalin rush. The majority of patients had a diagnosis of heart failure, pulmonary or lung disease, or liver disease.

I took the test for certification in ICU nursing. It was a difficult exam, but I loved to study. Nurses who took this exam had a wide knowledge base, and it helped when working with young hospital interns who had little experience. We guided them through different clinical situations so they wouldn't make any mistakes.

I loved teaching and was asked to teach many of the critical care courses for new arriving nurses into the ICU's. The assistant chief nurse said I was the most popular instructor and asked that I continue doing this course for new graduates. Many of those students wondered why I wasn't teaching nursing classes at the university.

Actually I did apply, but I was told I was the runner up. The faculty selected someone who had a four-year degree. I was a three-year diploma nurse before I went back to school to get a nursing degree. So consequently, I was told by my interviewer that my diploma school philosophy was not the same as that of the baccalaureate program. I didn't understand what she meant. I remember going back to our apartment that afternoon, lying down on the bed and crying. I really wanted that teaching job!

I had gone back to school to get my master's degree in nursing as well as going to the same university to get an art degree. Unfortunately, I was trying to achieve both of these degrees while I had many taxing responsibilities as the head nurse of the neurosurgery ward. It became too much for me to handle. Interestingly, Pete was understanding about my heavy workload and encouraging as well.

Not long after I moved in with Pete, I recall one summer morning we were sitting at the dining table in our apartment having breakfast. While looking through a magazine, waiting for Pete to finish eating before going off to work, I found a small ad that showed a pencil drawing of a dog. The caption said, " "Draw me!"

"I can do this!" I excitedly told Pete.

"You can do what?" he asked after sipping the last of his coffee.

"I can draw this little dog's face," I explained.

"Okay, show me," he said.

I did the drawing on a small piece of paper Pete provided along with one of his drafting pencils. I quickly rendered it. Pete was shocked.

"My, Susan. Why didn't you tell me you had this talent?" as he examined the drawing thoroughly.

I replied, "You never asked."

"Have you thought about going to art school? I can help you with your portfolio. I can assure you that if they don't accept you, they shouldn't accept anyone. You have a great talent!" he stated with pride.

This pleased me as I had begun to wonder about our relationship. But now he seemed to finally take notice of me. Being an artist himself made that approving gesture easy for him, I guess.

I was accepted into this prestigious school as he knew I would be. But I was so busy with my duties as a head nurse and taking statistics plus taking other nursing classes for my master's degree that I eventually dropped all of them.

Pete was saddened when I came home to tell him I dropped out of art school. But he gave me comfort as well. With tears in my eyes, he gave me a strong hug and expressed words of support for my decision. I continued to paint and draw in that small space we lived in. When I think back on that time, I can't imagine doing that. I painted with the canvas laying on my lap, while the palette of paint was positioned near me on the mattress covers. Pete's critiques of my painting were very helpful. He was an excellent artist, and I learned a lot from him. He seemed to be quite proud of my new skill.

While working in the ICU, I met many young medical students, and I became friends with several of them. After many long discussions a few of the students told me I should go to medical school. I did contemplate this for about a year, but I was over the age of thirty then and felt I was probably too old. But Pete also encouraged me to take the entrance exams. I seriously thought about it and thought my dad would be proud if I did become a physician, especially since he wanted that career but didn't get to fulfill that dream for himself.

However, I decided against this due to my dyslexia. Also, I didn't feel I had the confidence to take on the responsibility of being a physician. I didn't want a patient's death to be due to a judgement error on my part, which I had witnessed from some of our doctors. I think too, my mother's lack of support and love when I was a child caused me to have some degree of low self-esteem. After leaving home my confidence was building, but I still had those scars that never went away. Even though I loved my anatomy, physiology, and chemistry courses, I didn't think I would do well in math courses, another problem for dyslexics along with spelling. One of my cousins who was accepted to West

Point and had a long successful career in nuclear physics, told me he just worked around that disability. But it scared me, and not wanting to fail at any task, I erased that dream from my mind. Instead I decided to be the best nurse I could be.

CHAPTER FORTY

One day after working most of the afternoon taking care of a very critically ill patient, I found a few spare moments to take a break. I went into the nursing lounge, and within a few minutes, one of the other nurses came in to tell me she had a message for me. When she answered the nursing station phone the night before, the guy calling asked for me. She added that according to other nurses, he had called several times previously, trying to reach me.

"Susan, he said he was someone from your past," she smiled with that gaze of curiosity.

"Oh, really! Did he give his name?" I asked with much interest.

"No, but, he said to tell you to look in your unit mailbox here at the hospital for a letter that would be arriving soon," Karen answered.

Dear Susan,

By now you probably realize that I've been trying to call you at work. I just wanted to say "hello." It seems a shame to completely lose contact, and I felt the need to let you know that despite the "long time," I have not dropped off the face of the earth. I think I've made a bit of a pest of myself at MICU-1, hence the letter. I married Carol in May of 1990. Two teenage stepsons. Still live not far from where you visited me. I don't intend to cause any discomfort or embarrassment, and I certainly hope you're not angry. I only hoped to check in and see how life goes for you. Perhaps I'll leave further communication to you if you'd care to call or write. My address and number are here, and our e-mail address as well, but I suspect you haven't warmed up to daily computer use. You needn't feel uneasy about Carol; we're very open, and I have told her of you and of our rather unusual relationship.

 Take care.
 I hope all's well,
 Joe

Joe and I had not communicated for almost fifteen years. I don't remember how or why our correspondence dropped off, but his contacting me now was quite a surprise. As I read his letter, a feeling of sadness overcame me. I didn't want to feel jealousy when he announced he was married to a woman named Carol. I was married so why shouldn't he be happy in a new relationship; particularly sense I spurned his attention and affection during our military days. But I realized my feelings of endearment for Joe would never fade, so I decided to communicate with him on a regular basis. We wrote back and forth for several years after I married Pete. He knew I was not completely happy with my life, and during our correspondence, he often asked that I leave Pete. We even met twice when I traveled to New York to visit my father. We were very comfortable in each other's presence. But I believed in my wedding vows and leaving Pete was not in the equation, no matter how sad or empty I felt at times. I was truly afraid of what Pete might do to me, should I try to leave him.

FORTY-ONE

After reading his letter, I felt compelled to reread some of the correspondence we had years ago. I can't even explain to myself why I kept all his letters after marrying Pete. I think probably communicating with Joe filled a void somewhere deep down in my soul.

One envelope I received from him included not only his letter but also a copy of my previous letter to him. I remember that stirred my curiosity when I opened it those long years ago. The following is my letter to him and his reply to me.

Joe,

Thank you for writing. I'm glad you have recovered from your _____ with Barb. I left the blank space to indicate I didn't know how to describe your relationship with her.

Right now, I am envying your freedom. Your house purchase sounds very exciting! I wish I were in your shoes.

Joe, please excuse me for seeming "very unhappy" in my last letter.

I was concerned that I may have deepened your wounds.

Interestingly enough, however, that may have been my intent. If so, I now regret that. See, human behavior is so absurd! I really doubt that I can explain myself. But because, as you stated, "we are honest and straight forward with each other," I will try.

When I called you last August from my dad's house, I was hoping to set up a meeting with you in Pittsburg because I had a three-hour layover there on my return flight home. Instead, my ears were filled with your excitement about your new "young love." I realized that as your friend, I was supposed to be happy for you and I think I acted out my part quite well. As you talked, I told myself to remember your joy was to be expected someday. This is where the experiment comes into play, as our friendship has been an experiment for me. I wanted to see if we could really care for each other as "friends" are supposed to when other parties (persons) enter the picture. When I realized it was inappropriate for me to ask you to drive to Pittsburg, I felt saddened and confused. See, we "humans" are so selfish! Anyway, I went up to the bedroom and lied down for three hours. I felt a terrible emptiness! But after a while, I decided to view this situation as another learning experience. Why do I still want you to write to me? I think I know but don't want to reveal that to you. Anyway, I do have a request. I would like you to write only once a year on my birthday, which you always seem to remember since it's also your mom's birthday. I never receive presents on my birthday, so a letter from you telling me about all your year's experiences would be uplifting. Also, if a letter didn't arrive, I would call you to see if something was wrong. This may sound crazy to you, but it seems right to me.

You asked about artwork. I will send some this summer to your new address. You can make a comment or critique when you write to me in September. I dropped most of my art classes, acting on impulse as it was a particularly bad day for me. I felt sad doing that and remained somewhat tearful for several days. I may resume classes next fall. Currently, I'm trying to copy a few works by Sandro Botticelli, an artist I truly love. His sensitivity to human emotion is expressed better than any artist I've studied so far, and I would love my art to mimic his. Sadly, I don't have artistic genius as I feel Pete has. I may just be a "closet artist," but Pete continues to encourage me. I have done a lot of living in my thirty-three years, and with all the different emotions passing through me, I want to express them in my work.

I honestly believe that at the age of fifty, I will be living alone in a big house as a recluse, and at this point in my life, I am looking forward to that day.

I need to close so I hope you can understand me better now.

Good luck, Joe, in your practice of Law with your father. I'm also glad you are continuing to pursue your main talent of music! I will always love you for that.

Susan

Dear Susan,

The copy of your letter is enclosed because I wanted you to know my most recent impression of you. You've had six months to forget what was written, but it is all I know of you since then. I highlighted in pink just a few words that strike me most when I've re-read it. Also enclosed is a picture taken in December. Every few years or so I get restless and spend an evening snapping off a roll of self-portraits. A dubious tradition. I am very apprehensive about the tone in which I should write. For the past year or so, all I've done is get into trouble and get "scolded." First, there was the misunderstanding on the phone, Then that "wound-depressing" letter. Now I'm relegated to writing and being written to only once a year. And I haven't even done anything! I thought I made it clear the day you called from your dad's that Barb and I were not getting into anything permanent, or even serious. You must remember something. I really and truly don't even want to be married. Not ever. I remember sitting at the piano in your house in Denver and telling you that I had no faith in the matrimonial institution. I still most heartly feel that way.

Also, please remember that I live such an isolated existence as far as dating and romantic involvements are concerned that it's a real event just for me to have a date. This is not because I wouldn't like a date or involvement now and then, but because there are so few women (people) I find interesting, nice or worth the time and effort.

All this certainly doesn't mean that I can't care for someone or that I can't be hurt. All that happened last summer was a glimmer of light. I thought "hey, I might enjoy this – it might be good for both of us." The idea of marriage, seriousness or even mutual exclusivity was never really dreamed of. I thought I'd said all that over the phone. Perhaps I hadn't. The point is, though, that a meeting with you in Pittsburgh would have been great! I go to Pittsburgh often and at the drop of a hat. You have every right in the world to ask me to drive there. I can't for the life of me see how that would've been "inappropriate." My turn with Barb hadn't even begun to reach the point where I'd have to eliminate anything from my life much less my "relationship" with you. Even if we had continued seeing each other to the present time, I still can't see me passing up a chance to see you in Pittsburgh or indeed anywhere! Though I may have been enthusiastic, it was because I thought I'd found someone I liked. That's a far cry from changing my like – in any way.

Of course, now I regard Barb as a big mistake. I was hurt, and I felt bad for some time. But when I regained my objectivity, I could see how blind I'd been. It angered me to think that someone devious like her would touch my life at all, and to think that she got far enough to affect you also just angers me that much more. I mean she really is a selfish "user," and I hate the thought that she might be remembered for what she did to the way I can relate to you. I'm sorry for what you felt that day, but it was unnecessary.

Remember Judy? 1978? She was the one who had so many emotional problems. We discussed her when last we saw each other.... I don't recall your reacting the same way, or maybe you didn't say. Please keep in mind that from my point of view there have always been "other parties" in the picture. Except for maybe our first two nights (July 9 & 10, 1971), Pete was always there. For most of the time you have been married. That's "other parties" enough for me! I have no problem with just being "friends" and being glad for you when you are happy. That's really all I've been able to be to you. I think I could be more to you, and I'd like to do so, given the right circumstances, but I'd never actively attempt- anything that could even be faintly interpreted as trying to break-up a marriage. I'm not trying to affect your behavior but just tell you how I feel. I think I could accept a friendship or relationship with you in whatever terms you wanted. I'm a complete variable.

As you like it and all that! I (we) have done nothing wrong in how we've related toward each other; I don't believe that feelings can be wrong — or of themselves make "wrongness, however they appear to us. It's our behavior and what we do that can hurt or be wrong. Your idea of a "learning experience" seems to imply that

I've been a villain, that I've wronged you somehow and that you'd have been better off not to have been mixed-up with me. And I just can't see that that has been the case. Still, now it's like I'm being punished, and as though I deserved it.

I'm finding it rather difficult to express myself this way. Seems communication can so often depend on the slightest subtlety or inflection, and the written word just cannot capture that. What I'm leading up to is a serious proposal that we communicate by cassette tapes. Surely you have or can easily get or get access to a little cassette player. It really would be a much more reward medium of communication. It's so much more personal. This is especially true if we're only going to do this once a year. Please give it a good try.

Come back on tape. Besides all the logical reasons, I just like the sound of your voice and the way you talk. Please. We'd know each so much better and so much more easily and with much less chance of misunderstanding.

Just tonight I had an interesting experience, and I relate it to you only for its poignancy. As I was preparing to write you and looking for pictures, I came across some pictures of Jennifer.

Jennifer was a girl I'd known for just about two weeks in San Francisco, January 1978. (I remember writing to you that I'd had the misfortune of meeting her only two weeks before her already-planned move to New York). I don't know why – for I've come across the pictures like this before, several times – but, while looking at these pictures, I felt closer to her than ever. I got cold chills! I thought that here's a girl I'd known for only two weeks.

We saw each other often but not constantly. We'd taken the time to jump in Fargo, drive down the California coast, and we'd stopped at a beautiful spot overlooking the ocean where I'd taken her picture. The smile she's giving me is a warm one, and it reveals how close we were that day, and for that short time. Though I've only had one letter and a few calls (later that year) from her, and though I'd lost trach of her completely, I felt comfort in the thought that such things, such improbable pleasures can happen. Here was a girl who seemed to care for me as I was with all my eccentricities and foibles. Here was one who had no problem dealing with me, who trusted me and wanted to be there and share that moment by the ocean with me. Though I have doubts about what it would have been like had we been afforded more time, what time we had was good. I was so moved by the experience that I called her father – I'd threatened to do so several times before – even though I knew she didn't get on with him. As you know (from experience), I like to re-contact with people after having lost it. In this case, not by way of re-kindling any old flames but just to see how she was. Frankly, I'd feared for her prospects; and I felt she was headed for a tough time. Who knows, she may have been in dire straits for the past few years, but I suspect she is okay now. Her dad tells me that right now she's on her honeymoon in Paris and lives in L.A.. I left my number, perhaps she'll call.

Did I ever tell you where I keep your picture in my house?

It's hanging behind my bedroom door. I figure only people I know very well would ever see it. I planned it that way because I don't share knowledge about you with anyone, at least not lightly. It seems too intimate. Besides, I enjoy the fact that ours is an isolated relationship: we have no mutual acquaintances. Also, ours is a complicated relationship and a fortuitous one – it would be very difficult for one who doesn't know me well to understand. I suppose it really just comes down to selfishness – I don't want to share you. Private. Putting your picture out where all the traffic could see it would make me feel like a show-off.

I sat in my living room late last night and carefully regarded the pictures of my family on the wall. I thought of all the precious ties and heritage I have here in my hometown. But then that only made me think more fondly of my other chapters: Denver, Baltimore, Honolulu, and San Francisco. I thought of the goodness of those periods of my life as well. They were very real – though they may seem dreamlike now – and certainly as precious. I think that one of the tougher aspects of feeling a bit more "settled" now is that I'm out of school and working and will be holding on to all that, and I plan to work on it. Don't misunderstand – I don't expect to get "stuck" here. I hope to travel a good deal. But there are so many times that can never be appreciated fully again.

Let me make something else clear: I'm not a young ambitious, eager lawyer. I don't think about practicing law all the time. It's not really my top choice, as you know, and I'm not at all fired-up about it. I'll do it well enough to represent my clients, do a good job and all, but then I leave "lawyer" in the office. When I'm home I don't think about lawyering; I think about music and film and reading and reveling. Leisure. The most important thing about being a lawyer, to me, is that I'm on my own, and I can afford to take off when I want. No dreary routine if I don't want it.

In my spare time I don't like to tell "law" stories; I talk about other things. I don't socialize with any lawyers except my Dad and a friend who's still in law school but into film. Lawyers are boring.

So I'm not all psyched about a brand new budding legal career.

I do, however, feel good in general. Better than in a while.

Except for the fact that I'd like to have a girlfriend or at least someone to date every now and then, everything is going well for me. This is true basically because I'm independent, in my own place and not pressured. I refuse to let my life become hectic.

My house is an old (65-70 yrs.) white frame house with a porch and swing. It's plenty big for one person — a family of four was here before. It's white now but will be some outlandish,

San Francisco-style color in a few years when it needs a paint job.

And I'm having a fire chimney put on my fireplace. Warmth.

Atmosphere. Plenty warm for guests. Tennis courts next door. Not a great neighborhood but okay. Many kids. Walk to work. One room is a gallery for original works by people I know (broadly defined). No TV. Baby grand (of course).

Do you remember me telling you about the mellotron, the electronic keyboard? It's not an organ or synthesizer, but, without getting into technical explanations, it can sound like anything you want. Usually used for string and orchestra sounds, a la Moody Blues. I got one in July. Wanted one since Hawaii, very badly since San Francisco. It was my graduation, my finished - with - school- forever celebration. I love it. Mine does violins, brass and, get this, a choir. Just play a chord and four men and four women sing "Ahhhh....". It's great. It's loud and I play all the time!

I have gotten back behind my camera, and I'm working very slowly on a film. My sister and niece are my actresses. This'll take years, but I'm in no hurry. Also I've committed myself to trying to do the music for a film a friend's friend has done. Don't know how that will work. And I've consented to trying my mellotron out in church. The organist at our church is a real master, and I would really enjoy working with a musician of his stature. It should sound wonderful – the acoustics are good, and it's a big beautiful sounding pipe organ. To add the 'tron would make it celestial!

Well, I've gone on and on in a manner which befits an annual effort. I've tried to bring you up to date so I've concentrated on what I'm doing. It seems like a really self-centered letter, but such must be the nature of this type of yearly exchange: I tell you about me, and you tell me about you – all inquiries (what 'you been doin' – how you been... what'r you doin' now?") are understood. Right?

Obviously, I've decided to go along with your "write each other only on our respective birthdays" idea, but I'd also go back to a more frequent method if you feel different now. But that's up to you.

If you do really want to stick to the annual – letter idea, I think it would be a beautiful concession (in the spirit of 'give 'n take' and all) if you'd really make a strong effort to switch to tapes. Also please notice that I've chosen not to be upset about not receiving some drawings, though I think I might be justified if I were – your statement was definite.

I began thinking about this letter very heavily about a week ago. Its composition began to take shape in my head last Thursday or so, and I've spent two evenings setting this all down. I hope I've got the idea of how you want our correspondence to be. If not, please tell me.

I hope you are well in spite of what seemed (in your last letter) to be a sort-of-general depression. I really can't say that I understand why your sadness seems to persist. I would certainly be accommodating if you were to decide to be more definite, but I don't want you to feel that I'm trying to "squeeze" anything out of you.

You know that I've valued our relationship almost ineffably over the years, whatever you've seen fit to give me has been accepted gratefully and kept safe. I hope you realize that.

Believe me, I don't want to lose this.

Please take care of yourself... for both our sakes.

As always,

Joe

One afterthought:

I wish we could get to know each other in a way that would enable us to explore each other's humor more fully. But I wish many things....

CHAPTER FORTY-TWO

After reflecting on the times we corresponded over several years by letter, email and of course tapes, I wondered how my life would have been different if I had chosen to move to Joe's hometown when he asked all those years ago.

A few weeks after I received his letter at work, Joe called me. I took the call in our unit break room, where there was some privacy. We didn't have cellphones then, and the wall phone by the entrance door was used for personal calls for all of the nursing staff. Occasionally, someone would come in to get something out of their locker, or they used the restrooms located to the right of the door. But every one of us respected each other's privacy when we did have personal calls. A few weeks after our reconnection, I received this strange call from Joe.

"Susan, I can't take it any longer! I want out!" he said with frustration.

I was surprised to hear this from him as I thought he finally picked the perfect partner. He had sent pictures of them taken before they married. She was pretty, shorter than he, and from the letter attached he explained how his friends found her for him, thinking they were well suited for each other. She was a history professor at the local college. She had been married and as he mentioned in his correspondence, her two young sons were present when they took their vows. He always loved children, and I knew he would enjoy raising them with her.

"Joe, I can't believe you are saying this! I thought you met your perfect mate. What about her sons? You love them, and you love her. How can you say now that you want out?" I asked with surprise.

His reply was, "Carol has seven cats! There were ten and they are all over the place! They used to go in and out of the house, but after two of them were sadly poisoned with antifreeze somewhere in the neighborhood, the rest no longer have the freedom to go outdoors. My creativity is buried under these jumping little creatures! I can't stand looking at them anymore. As far as the boys are concerned, they are grown now and off to college, so they don't need my guidance anymore. I want my privacy back and I need my space! I can't create music with this chaos in the house!"

I felt so sad for Joe as I listened to his frustration. I thought he now had a happy fulfilling life with the woman who would make him happy and content. Maybe for most of the ten years of their marriage, she did. But I knew he was serious and really wanted out of their marriage. Leaving my jealous feelings aside, I tried to talk him into seeing the good life he had with Carol, even though I had never met her or witnessed their time together. I wanted to keep the conversation going long enough to change Joe's mood and decision. But, unfortunately, it was shortened when my thirty-minute supper break ended.

I relayed our brief conversation to a dear nursing friend. She was a good listener and offered advice on many occasions. She was the only person who knew of my unique relationship with him over these many years. I did not tell her how my life with Pete was giving me many tearful restless nights of sleep or how we lived. Nor that his verbal and physical abuse became more frequent and more violent as the years passed. I tried conveying some of that to Joe in my letters, but he didn't really know about the abuse; he only knew of the depression. And from his letter, he didn't understand where it was coming from. I was afraid if I told him my story, as he told me his story with Carol that he would come out and confront Pete. I was afraid that Pete would probably kill him.

Twenty years ago computer use was foreign for many. But all the medical staff were sufficiently instructed on how to enter notes and lab results on patient's charts. Most of our staff physicians were hesitant and quite reluctant to switch from paper charting to computer charting, but eventually they realized the benefits.

Joe, having learned some computer skills, was surprised to learn that I was proficient in using one as well, even though I didn't have a computer at home. So, we started emailing each other on a regular basis- sometimes daily. But sometimes our emails stretched out a month before receiving a return reply.

He enjoyed reminding me of our first meeting while we were both in the military. His recollection was a bit different from mine, but he did have a better memory than me. The following remembrance is as follows:

I phoned you out of the clear blue on Tuesday evening, July 6, 1971. Monday had been a holiday because July 4th was on that Sunday. I had tried to call you Monday evening, but I had the wrong number (remember, they were 5-digit numbers for the on-post phone system). My personnel records boss had gotten me your correct number.

I was in one of those big, wooden phone booths in the lobby of the hospital.

We ended up talking for over an hour..............but, before we'd talked for ten minutes, you asked how you could meet me (I was [wasn't?] ready for that).

It was in that conversation that I mentioned the guy who'd told me about you felt the common perception was that you were "into" classical music (not current stuff). You said he probably thought that because your favorite piece was "Rhapsody in Blue." I then proceeded to tell you how that (and Gershwin in general) had always been a favorite of mine and one of my better accomplishments as well. So you knew that before we ever met face-to-face.

Also, in that conversation, you told me the number of your mailbox and that you would be working 10-6 the following

Friday, July 9, 1971. I told you that I'd find you somewhere between the hospital and where you lived. So it wasn't really a surprise to you that I'd be turning up while you were walking home. You just didn't know exactly when or where. Heck, it was almost a date!

You fooled me a bit because, when you came down to check your mailbox, you just looked in (I guess there was nothing there) and didn't open it. Just then some guy said something to you, and you were distracted. You sort of replied but then went on out of the lobby without opening the box. I was still pretty sure it was you but a bit insecure about it. Remember that I'd gotten your description from Eddie who hadn't seen you in a while. He didn't know you wore wigs and that he'd never seen your real hair or that you had FIVE wigs! He'd been very confused about the color and style of your hair (no bloody wonder)!

You chided me for having a moustache: "Everybody had a moustache." A few weeks later, out of deference (memory) for you, I shaved it.

By the end of our conversation, somebody's little dog had visited your apartment and was sitting on your lap.

We hit if off pretty well for total strangers.

Now, Friday, July 9, 1971. What happened? Who did what? Who said what to whom? Whose idea was it to go to the piano? How many wigs you wore. All that and more...................

I called you that afternoon, fearing you had changed your mind about our date.

You hadn't.

We went off to see "Summer of '42".........at the Cooper on South Colorado Blvd.

We didn't even get out of Fargo because there was a ridiculously long line. Probably never would've gotten in.

Now I'm not sure how we decided which way to go or what to do. I think we might have just been driving around. My instinct might have been to head to Larimar Square because I liked to hang out there.

But we didn't get that far. We ended up at (Cheesman or was it Chessman?) Park. At the outdoor stage, they were doing a dress rehearsal of a pretty big production of "Guys and Dolls." I remember Robert Q. Lewis was playing Nathan Detroit. I'd seen the play at college a few years earlier (and had seen the movie), so I was pretty familiar with it.

We sat on the wall surrounding a fountain or some decorative pool kind of thing and watched most of the show. But we were far enough away that we could carry on a conversation without bothering anyone. So I think we talked mostly. You had read our respective horoscopes for that day. Mine was that I shouldn't get involved with _____ (I forget who or what). In my mind, I used that as evidence that you really liked me.

It was a nice, warm evening, and after the show, we weren't ready to go home yet. So, at my suggestion, we headed for the Vogue Theatre near the University of Denver. The object was to see the "underground" films that showed at midnight. This had been another of my habits.

As we approached the neighborhood, you meekly said, "I don't think I want to go" This, I'm pretty sure, was a reaction to the neighborhood, Bohemian and hippie-like.

Anyway, I think then we just went back to your quadrangle and sat and talked for a few hours. It was really serious talk. Lots of confidences and such. You told me all about your mother's illness. We were the only ones there.....no hordes of traffic like we'd had the evening before.

I stayed too long, I'm quite sure.

I left thinking we'd be going out the next night and that things had gone very well and that our prospects were good as well.

When I called on Sunday, the 11th, you told me "not tonight and not this week." I called a week later and got the brush off. That was that. What a meanie!!

See there?

Joe

Here is Joe's recollection of another subject. This email was dated October 20, 2000:

I'm writing at work (where, till now, it's been a hectic week) on Friday morning......the 20th. It was thirty years ago today that I went into the Army. I've had my beard over half my life! I really don't know what I look like!.

I had an idea (and I'll try to shorten this). This occurred to me mostly because we don't know any of the same people, and only a few of my friends even know you exist:

A few other guys and I meet three or four times a year (if we're lucky). We have dinner, drink wine, play pool or watch movies or play music. Been doing it for years. We call it "chowder" but not because of what we eat........

We're big on telling stories. Though we've been friends for years (some back to childhood - - two of them are cousins), I've never shared the story of how you and I met or that I even knew you or had a long-standing acquaintance with you.

They would be surprised that they didn't know about you because we know just about everything about each other (you know, small town, same schools, know the families). They would have known about most of my ""girlfriends" at least back in the mid-70's. We've been to the same parties, picnics, and such, and I've known all their significant others, probably better than they've known mine.

Anyway (I'm getting carried away), we're doing chowder on November 10. I'd like to spend the evening telling them our story..........sort of in chapters and, hopefully, summarized a little more neatly than I'm doing with this now.

I could tell them about Denver.......then we play pool.......tell them how I found you several years later in another city and state........then we eat........and so on............

I really think it's a great story......you know, meeting in such a silly fashion at such a young age but still staying in contact in spite of so many interruptions.

Good story, but the finale (that I wouldn't tell them about until just before) would be to call you and let you just say "Hi" to them.

Just a thought..........what do you think?

His email of February 21, 2002, is as follows:

A bit of bother has developed here..........I've been diagnosed with multiple myeloma.

Going to need chemo.

I'll be doing 4-day stints in the hospital (starting tomorrow) every 3 or 4 weeks for nearly a year.

We've been pretty worried for the last week when the possibility was raised, but now that we know what we're dealing with, Carol and I feel much better. The worst thing I felt was hating the possibility of leaving her all alone.

Anyway, we're pretty upbeat now......no need for too much seriousness. The Dr. says that my otherwise healthy state is a big plus in reaching remission.

Of course, I'd never refuse prayers.

I didn't expect this, but I'm surely going to deal with it. I think I have a good shot at recovery.

Beware if you start surfing............some of the information on web sites about this malady are pretty grim......my Dr was much more optimistic.

So I'm off to my first inpatient stay since 1958......should be a trip.

Hi Susan,

I really appreciate your call and emails. Your phone message brought tears to my eyes. Tears have erupted quite a bit since I got sick and started telling everyone.

I was in the hospital (where I can't do email) from Friday (22nd) til yesterday (27th).....my first bout of chemo. All went well. I feel fine. No real symptoms.

Evidently, they caught it early (I apologize if I've already recited some of this......I've forgotten what I've told whom).

..........if my marrow is purified, I get a bone marrow transplant with my own marrow......pretty wild. That would be the beginning of my "cure"......which, of course, I would hope to continue. I'm sure I'll be very closely monitored.

The doctors are optimistic because I don't have any bone weakness (another indication of an early catch) or other serious pain or nausea.

I get to continue my usual lifestyle (volleyball, jet ski, Nordic Track, walking , carrying logs). The "usual routine" is encouraged as is an upbeat attitude. So I think there's every reason for high hopes.

My work schedule won't suffer too much because the hospital visits will be over weekends.

And yes, all indications are that I'll lose all my hair, including beard, moustache, and brows. Bummer. They say it comes back different. Don't know how I'll deal with that.......I know there will be no cosmetic tricks like wigs or tattoos. Just depends on how and how fast it comes out and how ugly or patchy it looks. Haven't seen myself since a few weeks before I turned up at your midnight shift in 1973. May be a shock!!!

So that's where I am. Probably frequent blood checks and such.

But I feel good. The symptoms which alerted me are gone, and I'm most happy about that. I no longer feel like winter is just driving me down and like I'm too weak to want to do anything. I feel basically normal.

I need to call you soon, and I will.............at work.

Take care, and many thanks again for your concern........I think I can make it through this.

Joe

Another email dated March 10, 2002:

I think it's kind of cute that you can't remember my birthday, but it's the 6th.

Carol's is today (she's 50).

I've been running on very low energy......if it wasn't absolutely necessary, I wouldn't do it. That's basically why I don't respond to emails as quickly as I'd like.

I'm feeling OK, but sometimes just can't get moving. Saturday was such a nice day, and I felt great.........sitting outside working on my laptop. Then yesterday cold and windy and awful. I hate this.

And, of course, I did get your card; you were right.......it says a great deal in just a few words.

Take care.

Joe

March 13, 2002, email from me to Joe:

Joe,

You will be receiving a message from my sister today. Please, please read it!!!!!!!!!!!!!! .....her boss had been diagnosed with multiple myeloma several years ago, and he is in complete remission. He is very intelligent and decided he didn't want to accept the conventional therapy. He has many friends as physicians, and he did research on other options. Anyway, I want you to talk to him. Please!!!!!!!

I don't want to alarm you, but your current chemo regime is too much! ....

You want to be here for Carol, and I want that for you too!! So, please open my sister's message. I may try to call you in a few minutes.

This is important, Joe. —Susan

Two days later I sent an email to his home:

Joe,
...............I don't mean to sound "frantic", but I am!! I want you to be here for many years!!! You need to be there for Carol, and I want you to write my biography twenty years from now!

You didn't take that "CHICKEN SOUP" as I told you to do.

While at work I replied to your message, so if you don't know what this is about, read that reply, too.

Take care, Joe. I'm trying to get you better. Really!!! I'm running with that umbrella!!! (the card)

Bye now.......Susan

Several weeks had passed and I was becoming concerned. I hadn't received any more letters or phone calls from Joe. He had given me his phone number which I never used, since it was his home phone. I didn't know how Carol would react to my calling, even though Joe said I didn't need to worry since she knew of our unusual friendship. Now, I decided I had to make that call to ease my mind.

"Hello," I said softly and slowly with some trepidation.

"Hello, is this Susan?" came the return voice.

"Yes, is this Carol?" I asked with some disquietude.

As a nurse, and having taken care of patients with this diagnosis, I wasn't feeling as optimistic as Joe. This cancer affects the white plasma cells of the body which produce antibodies. Joe probably went for that doctor's appointment because he was experiencing back pain or bone pain. Also affected by this type of cancer is kidney disfunction, anemia, and infection. The outcome did not look good from my perspective.

"Oh, Susan, I was planning to call you, but it has been so hectic around here. I am so sorry to let you know, but Joe passed away two weeks ago," she replied while waiting for my recovery and response.

Not able to hold back my tears, I returned with my condolences and continued by asking what happened.

"He went back into the hospital to receive the second dose of chemotherapy. His kidneys shut down, so he had to receive dialysis. The next morning, he had a cardiac arrest. They couldn't revive him. I know this is a terrible shock to you, Susan. I will tell you that the funeral was beautiful and over 200 friends and family attended. Joe was loved by so many," she continued trying to reassure me that he lived a blessed life.

The anguish I felt was almost unbearable. After saying "thank you" and "goodbye," I just sat there in the chair next to the phone in the unit lounge and cried. No one was in the room at the time. I didn't know if I could continue working my shift that evening, but fortunately my dear friend Gail was also working. I felt I had to confide in someone, and I was so glad she was able to take some time to listen to me. I remember standing in the hallway outside the doctor's lounge telling her, through a flood of tears, what had happened to Joe. Some of the physicians who passed by looked with dismay at my sudden change in demeanor. One or two asked if I was okay.

I cried all the way home. I had to hide my tears and reddened face from Pete. Fortunately, he was working in the back part of the building on a car. I called out to him that I was going straight to bed. I didn't see him until that next morning when I had recovered somewhat. Over several days, I would break down and start to cry. It was so difficult to keep from revealing my emotions to Pete, especially since we lived in such small open quarters. I felt so alone with my grieving. But I finally managed to tell him that a good friend of mine had passed away from cancer.

I was upset with Carol for not telling me about Joe's condition earlier as I would have found some way to go to his funeral. That would have given me some closure. But none of his family and only a few of his friends knew about me. Carol might have not wanted me there, especially having to explain who I was, if "friend" was not sufficient. If their marriage was crumbling as Joe seemed to reveal from our one phone conversation two years prior, then she would be hesitant to introduce me to anyone. He never got around to mentioning "our story" to the "chowder gang."

I did write to Joe's mother, expressing my condolences as well as telling her how great her son was in so many ways and how much I cherished our friendship. I didn't expect to get a return letter, but surprisingly she did write back. She knew that Joe sent me tapes of his compositions. Sadly, he had written one piece and asked me to give it a title. Unfortunately, I never did. She wanted copies of his music, which he never provided for her. After sending these to her, we corresponded a few more times. I sensed it helped her with his loss as it did me. Her daughter wrote to let me know when she passed not long after our last correspondence. She was ninety-two. I wish I had met Joe's family when he asked me thirty years earlier.

I didn't know one could love two people simultaneously, as I believed I did. Joe and Pete were so different in character and talent. But they deeply touched my heart, especially Joe. I had to heal my wounds and proceed with my life. I remember one day telling Joe on tape that I had a vision of me working in my flower garden in front of the house. After reaching the age of eighty I saw him drive up the road to greet me in his beloved Fargo. We both laughed.

A great mind was lost forever. My dear friend was gone, and I sadly didn't get to say goodbye.

With tears in her eyes, Cyndi gave me a hug and said, "Oh my, Mrs. Farwell. What a beautiful and yet sad love story!"

CHAPTER FORTY-THREE

Over the course of our marriage, Pete and I discussed divorce a few times. But neither of us actually left. By the end of the day after much quarreling, we cried together and let our differences go. Through the years we realized we couldn't separate because of our financial entanglement. We just accepted each other's foibles and went on.

His relationship with his family became more strained as the years went by. He wouldn't even speak to his father after one phone call where his father told him, "Pete, you are ridiculous!"

He didn't travel after encountering a few business or home break-ins. His parents were too old to come visit, so when I could, I would visit them without Pete. On holidays I would call his father after his mother died, but Pete never engaged in the conversation. His brother and sister stopped seeing him, and when they did communicate it was a short conversation. Pete really did love his siblings, and as the oldest he felt he should always be their protector. He strong convictions and comments about numerous topics, however, often offended his listeners. That included his brother and sister; they just stopped listening, even though they both agreed Pete was the genius in the family.

Everyone in Pete's family and all of his friends thought Pete would achieve the greatest success in life. But as with most families, disappointment creeps in eventually. Pete struggled with his career and didn't become the great designer that everyone thought he would be. His brother, who didn't excel in school and loved sports instead, became a vice-president of a large manufacturing company and married a very successful lawyer. They accumulated much wealth as did Pete's sister and her husband, who eventually owned his own manufacturing company.

Pete never said he was envious of their accomplishments. He just continued working as much as he could and still dreamed big dreams! I also encouraged these dreams of his; I wanted him to become that person I admired when we were in the military. I knew he was different from anyone else I had known; I liked his determination, fire, and pride!

After about ten years of living together and Pete not getting satisfaction from working for design firms, he directed his attention to car restoration. He left the design artistry behind. I was sad about that, but his love of cars and his meticulous care of them, gave him great pleasure. He loved welding, sanding, and painting, all of which were required to restore old automobiles. His attention to detail had customers coming back. So he did have an adequate income along with mine to buy the things he wanted. Unfortunately, he didn't allow me that same option. That was when our many troubles began.

CHAPTER FORTY-FOUR

Pete had what was called the "Midas touch." Everything he touched turned to "gold," a phrase passed down through the centuries in reference to King Midas of Greek mythology who loved gold!

I felt fortunate that Pete had this ability, but he used it to his advantage and not to mine. He knew when the value of something would increase overtime, and he would decide when to buy and when to sell. He never invested in the stock market because he felt it was too risky. He always said he would put money in gold if we had money to spare. But, we didn't. He also told his friends and me, "The best outcome financially is to invest in yourself."

When he wasn't working, Pete was reading. He had a few lawyer friends, who felt he was much smarter than they were. One family friend of his parents' who was president of the state bar association wanted Pete to become a lawyer and go into practice with him. But Pete felt lawyers were part of the cause for the downfall of our country. The son of that lawyer, who did go into practice with his father, told Pete that while in law school he learned there was no difference between right and wrong. Pete was shocked!

Pete had high moral values. He was very honest, and his customers appreciated that as did I. I never worried that he would have an affair. Over the years his old girlfriend would call a few times after she divorced her husband. That bothered me, but he said she was too crazy for him.

I remember coming home from working the day shift one Sunday afternoon and found a friend of Pete's sitting in the living room with him listening to music by "Chicago." Pete introduced her to me and said they had gone horseback riding early that day. She was pretty with long blond hair and was two years older than Pete. He was friends with her and her husband, although I had never met either one of them. I didn't feel jealous as I might have expected, but when he told me after she left that she wanted him to go to a "Chicago" concert with her, I said, "No!"

They didn't go, and he realized if we were to remain together, he had to remain faithful. He had no problem with that as he loved me as I loved him. He told me often how beautiful I was, and we both realized over the years how much we had in common. Our interests included the love of art, music, religion, and politics which kept our conversations going for hours.

Many friends would ask, "How do you find the time to talk with each other?"

Many couples I knew said they didn't even talk over dinner, and they probably spent just fifteen minutes a day talking together. How sad I thought. Pete and I could spend hours and hours a day discussing so many issues. Since we didn't have children, that made it easier of course. Usually, he expounded on topics that he was very knowledgeable about and that piqued my interest. I learned so much from him, as did his friends. Sometimes after arriving home from work, I noticed Pete's voice would be hoarse from talking hours on the phone with his friends. They loved listening to his views about how to make money and about politics. I was happy he had these friends, and I was proud that they were spellbound by his accomplishments and his general knowledge of so many things. He had been a good student in high school and college. His best friends went on to have careers in the FBI, CIA, and finance. He could have as well, but he decided to pursue his love of art and design.

If we had had children, I think they would have been very intelligent, and handsome. But, sadly with our life as it was, they would have probably had mental issues as well. We couldn't have raised a child in the living space we called home for over thirty years. Plus, in hindsight, I don't believe Pete would have given them the attention they needed.

I often thought many people didn't take into consideration all the responsibilities of raising a child. My grandfather from Denmark left home when he was only eight years old due to abuse from his stepmother, according to information handed down to us. Many children of that era had to leave home for several reasons. Some left to find work to help support the family, some left because there was not enough food available for them to even survive, and some left because of the parental abuse.

When Pete had his angry outbursts, he would say, "Now don't analyze me, dam it!"

Sometimes I wondered if his enraged behavior was due to the cycle of the moon. In the medical field, we noticed that mothers had their babies more often when there was a full moon. Also the psyche patients acted more erratically than usual during that time. His malice towards me seemed to come about every six months. I didn't keep a journal, but it did seem to occur at regular intervals. I felt fortunate this ebullition didn't come more frequently.

Using some of my psychological probing, I learned from Pete that one day at the end of the Korean War, he and his younger brother were playing on the living room floor. After being away from home for over a year as a Captain in the Marine Corps, his father suddenly entered the house. For an unknown reason to Pete, instead of greeting him and his brother with a loving hug and kiss, he leaned down and slapped Pete across the face!

"What in the world would have made your father do this?" I asked in astonishment!

Pete calmly answered, "I don't know. I must have done something wrong, I guess."

Pete and his father never got along after he left for college. His dad, a lover of sports, wanted Pete to become a football star, like so many fathers dream for their sons. Pete was physically built for athleticism. In high school and college the coaches were upset he didn't go out for sports. One coach said he could throw a perfect spiral football like none of the other guys, and he was frustrated Pete didn't take an interest and sign up for the team. Even with his strong musculature, he could run fast! One or two of his cousins had college track records for running. They all decided it must have been in their DNA! He also loved ice skating! He could skate backwards as well as forwards, and the hockey coaches were equally frustrated he didn't take up that sport either.

His response to them was simply, "I am not interested in team sports."

He wanted to accomplish endeavors on his own without help from anyone else. He told me that as a small six-year-old child, he asked his father if it would be possible for one person to build a large house by himself. Of course, his father said, "No!"

That was his intention with our home. He did try to complete it without any help from anyone. It was an 8000 sq. ft. structure, and he designed it for business and home as I mentioned earlier. It was a beautiful design, but over the years, Pete came to realize he couldn't finish it by himself. After his mother passed away, he lost interest and the structure fell into ruin.

I believe his own frustration and feeling of failure in this project caused him to take out his anger on me. When he would begin to throw things about and start raising his voice, I knew to remain quiet and calm so as not to escalate the situation. I learned this from my nursing training for dealing with combative patients.

Pete would get close to my face and scream profanities at me! Everything was my fault! His pupils would enlarge, and his facial expression looked like he was possessed by the Devil! Sometimes he would grab me, push me up against the refrigerator, and squeeze his strong hands around my neck until I almost couldn't breathe. Fortunately, he would release his grip before I passed out or died from asphyxiation. When I cried, he didn't seem to be concerned. He was satisfied that he had made his point clear. One day during his calmer moments, I asked him why he treated me this way. His reply was, "It makes me feel good." I knew he needed counseling, but I could never broach the subject with him. And as most abused victims, I didn't confide in anyone. I tried to hide it.

Many victims have low self-esteem. I mentioned that my mother didn't provide me with love and encouragement when I was a child, and consequently, I suffered from low self-esteem. When Pete said something was my fault, I accepted the blame.

There were times when I thought Pete would kill me! I don't know why he didn't unless his love for me repressed his will to destroy me.

CHAPTER FORTY-FIVE

After a little research and reading, I learned that abusers want power over their victims.[55] Nearly twenty people per minute are abused by their partner. There are more than ten million incidents of domestic abuse reported each year, and sadly, that statistic continues to rise! This abuse occurs usually behind closed doors, and often the violent abuse follows verbal abuse. The abuser tries to prevent their partner from seeing their family or friends. Alcohol and drugs are contributing factors in many abuse cases. Abusers are often bullies but feel powerless. They want control over their victim.

There are many typical profiles to categorize an abuser, but for Pete I believe needing to be right and in control were the main factors that led him to become abusive. His personal achievements and dreams couldn't be reached. As the realism of certain constraints beyond his control interfered with him achieving these dreams, his defense mechanism was to take his frustration out on me and control me.

One evening Pete came home very late from an outing with a friend to hear a lecture given by a military combat pilot. I then made the mistake of saying I was concerned about when he would get the building finished, not wanting to believe we would be spending the rest of our lives living in this very untidy confining space. His reaction was explosive! He yelled and then slapped me hard across my face! My left eye started to swell immediately, and I think this surprised him as well. At least that was what I wanted to believe if he truly loved me. I had to work the next

---

55   Darlene Lancer, JD, LMFT, "The Truth About Abuser, Abuse, and What to Do," https://www.psychologytoday.com June 6, 2017

day. I didn't want to go as I was afraid how my face would look. I didn't want to have to explain how this occurred, and I didn't want this abuse to be exposed! I knew the swelling would get worse, even though I immediately put ice on it. I also knew it would become ecchymotic or black and blue as well. I hoped my eye socket bones had not been fractured, or worse, that I could lose my eyesight!

Without showing concern for my injury, he replied with, "Tell your co-workers that one of the 2x4's I was lifting onto the roof swerved from a gust of wind and hit you in the face."

Wow! As I tried to sleep, I did a lot of praying that night, asking to be removed from this nightmare!

One of Pete's friends who ended the friendship because he experienced abuse from him as well, commented to me years later that Pete told him he would kill me if I left him. I wasn't surprised to hear this; in fact, I came to believe it myself and possibly that was one reason I stayed in the marriage. I knew of restraining orders being issued by the courts to keep abusers at a designated distance from their intended victims. But I also read reports where this legal injunction didn't always work. Very scary!

One summer afternoon I went down our winding road through the large, wooded forest to get the mail. Instead of the mail, I was surprised to find a magazine in our mailbox that hadn't been put there by our mailman. On the cover was the title of an article within the magazine about mental and physical abuse. My initial reaction was embarrassment; someone from the outside world knew about Pete's abuse towards me. Suddenly, I felt ashamed, and immediately I wondered who sent this magazine. Was someone anonymously trying to warn or help me? Someone, either a friend or maybe even a customer of Pete's, realized I was in danger. Maybe someone stopped by to see Pete and heard the yelling and physical abuse coming from behind those walls. Or perhaps someone from work didn't believe my story about the 2x4. I was afraid to read the information. I think I threw the magazine away, not wanting Pete to see it and learn he had been found out. I worried what action he might take. As with most victims, I repressed my own fears as I waited for the next surprise attack.

CHAPTER FORTY-SIX

Life wasn't always difficult or frightening with Pete. He often made me laugh, and we shared our dreams of building a beautiful house on our twelve acres of woods. Whenever Pete would find a small sapling from his favorite tree, the oak, he would call me to come out and look at it as he took my hand and guided me through the woods. He loved the shadows made by tall trees when the moon was full. He knew the names of all our trees. I said he was a "tree hugger." To this day, I appreciate that beauty as well.

He loved the night sky and using his telescope he would show me the planets, constellations, shooting stars, and eclipses.

We had great horned owls and barn owls living in our woods, and while sipping his evening coffee, he loved listening to their calls back and forth. He would suddenly say, "Do you hear them?"

We loved going to art museums when he could spare the time and we could find a "house sitter" to stay at our place while we were away. I remember one visit to the city museum to see a temporary exhibit of Jean Auguste-Dominique Ingres works. From my art history classes I loved looking at the pictures of Ingres paintings in art books. The detailing was so impressive. As I mentioned before, he became one of my favorite artists.

After we viewed the massive Ingres paintings and Pete explained many details of his work, we went into another area of the museum to see a permanent collection of artists' works. I noticed Pete stood for the longest time looking at a self-portrait of Rembrandt. When I walked over to ask why he was looking at it so intently, his reply surprised me.

"This is not Rembrandt's work!" he stated with some dismay and explained why this was so.

We found out several weeks later that indeed it was not a Rembrandt painting! The museum must have been horrified at that purchase. What an error!

Because I couldn't keep my car in the unfinished garage since there was no room, he would always start the engine to warm the car and clean off the windshield before I went to work on cold, snowy winter days. Even during the warmer months, he made sure I had a clean windshield.

He would say, "Bo, you always need clean car windows. They are the windows to your world."

I wasn't really sure what he meant, but I liked that message. He was meticulous about having clean vehicles, and he loved collecting automobiles that increased in value over time. Unfortunately, most of my income was used to purchase them. His income was used for building materials for the huge structure called home. It was a compromise.

His greatest dream was to produce a car for the streets that looked and had the speed of a race car. He loved the DeLorean automobile designed by John DeLorean, an American engineer, inventor, and executive of the U.S. auto industry. DeLorean developed the Pontiac GTO and the Firebird, both very popular cars when we were young. Pete wanted to emulate DeLorean. He spent hours during the evening working on his own car designs. I thought they were beautiful!

Because of mutual interests, Pete became friends with an older man who spent his career designing parts, specifically a transmission, for General Motors. After he retired, he continually worked in his shop at his home on perfecting engine performance. One day he asked Pete to help with a mechanical design flaw. Within two or three days, Pete found the solution. Sadly, his friend, who was in his nineties by this time, passed away suddenly before Pete could tell him his discovery!

Our property soon had a collection of old cars! They were in the interior of the building and around the perimeter. Being a Virgo, I became frustrated with the appearance of junk everywhere. But Pete insisted he needed these vehicles for "parts" when he did repairs. He loved engines and had three huge engines mounted on square wooden blocks in his shop. They were works of art to him!

An older man and friend of Pete's had a tool and dye company. After he retired, Pete decided he wanted to buy many pieces of machinery that were used in the process of tooling and dying. They were extremely heavy, cumbersome, and huge, and were delivered while I was at work. They took up almost one third of the floor space in the shop which was about 4000 sq. ft..

To my surprise, Pete used all of these complicated pieces of equipment when he fabricated parts for customers' vehicles. He did wonderful work with great precision! He was proud and loved showing me his finished products. There was a large sheet metal cutter, a lathe, and several others. I don't recall what they were used for, but Pete did. I wondered where he received all this knowledge; it wasn't from his father.

I think that was part of the reason he and his father didn't get along. Once early in our relationship when we visited his family for the Christmas holidays, he was angry with his dad because the front doorknob was loose on his parent's house. There were no locks on the door either. Pete was furious! He told his dad that he should have the house secure and safe, especially for his mom when she was home alone.

He and his mother had a great relationship. He was her favorite child of three. He was the oldest, the smartest, and the best looking. He looked like her, and he inherited her intelligence as well. When she slowly succumbed to Alzheimer's disease, he lost his world as well. As I mentioned earlier, his brother, sister, and father showed little respect for him as the years passed. They were angry that he didn't provide a home for us, so they stopped coming to visit and eventually stopped calling.

I remember one morning Pete started to cry as he told me about a dream he had had the night before. He said he saw his younger brother - a small child in the dream - riding his bicycle on the roof of a house when suddenly the wheels got caught in the gutters. He fell from the roof as Pete was looking up from the ground and trying to warn his brother to be careful. Pete cradled his brother's limp body in his arms and cried. So sad!

CHAPTER FORTY-SEVEN

It seemed every year in our city there was an auto show. Pete loved going to these and tried never to miss them. Usually someone, if not me, then a friend, also a lover of cars, would go with him. However, on this particular day, he went alone. It was a beautiful Saturday in March. He spent hours walking through that massive building looking at all the innovations on car design and engine performance. The exhibiters were numerous and offered so much information for Pete to consume. Every year he would bring home bags of literature. He read all the handouts and tried to incorporate concepts from this information into his own car design.

He arrived back home late that afternoon, after leaving around 8:00 that morning. He looked tried, and when he came in and sat down in his chair, he told me he had to park the car several blocks from the convention building. He said he had to stop several times to catch his breath.

Pete was always so proud of his strength and physique, so I was a little surprised when he told me this. When I encouraged him to make an appointment to see the doctor on Monday, he said, "I feel fine now." He hated going to doctors, but I finally convinced him, and he made the call early Monday morning. Fortunately, after he explained his symptoms from Saturday they set up the appointment that day. Since he always wanted the property guarded, he wouldn't allow me to go with him. A few hours later I received a phone call from Pete.

"Bo, the nurse drove me over to the hospital next to Dr. Kent's office to have a cardiac catheterization. They admitted me after the procedure, and I am talking to you from my room now. The cardiologist told me I had a heart attack Saturday, so they put in two stents, and I have to stay here for a few days. I don't want you to worry; I feel fine. I want you to stay home and continue to guard the place. We can't afford to have someone break-in while you are here with me. Do you understand? I will be okay and will come home in a few days. I love you!"

Suddenly I felt a wave of nausea. Immediately I thought why did I not take him to the emergency room that Saturday evening! He hadn't experienced chest pain — only shortness of breath, but I should have considered the possibility of an infarction.

"I love you, Pete," I said as tears welled up in my eyes. I didn't want to sound fearful and give him cause for alarm. He seemed content that he was going to get better after the catheterization. I wanted to know which coronary artery was occluded that required the stents, but, Pete didn't know.

After hanging up the phone, I spent the rest of the day crying as I feared the worst! With my dog sitting by my side, I sat in Pete's chair and wept until I feel asleep.

By Tuesday morning, I knew I needed to be at the hospital with Pete. No wife would just stay at home. How terrible! So I called one of our friends who had stayed at our place several times before. Fortunately, he was not working and said he could come over around noon. I wanted to allay Pete's fears by having someone at the property while I was gone.

The hospital was only five miles away. When I arrived, I stopped at the nursing station in the Coronary Care Unit. Each patient had a private room, and I was directed down the short corridor to room number 217.

I stood at the entrance door, and happily saw Pete wearing a hospital gown, sitting in a chair next to his bed, watching TV. Not wanting to startle him, I spoke before entering the room. He looked up and smiled!

After giving him a hug and kiss, he said, "My God, Bo! When I saw you standing in the doorway, I thought you were an angel! I couldn't believe you were really here!"

He was so happy I came. Of course, I had to explain that Matt was staying at our place, so he wouldn't have to worry.

By Wednesday, he was back home. He was supposed to have another stent placed six weeks later, but because he was feeling better, he didn't have that done. I tried to convince him to follow doctors' orders and get that procedure, but his stubbornness prevailed. Thankfully, he did take his cardiac medications.

CHAPTER FORTY-EIGHT

Pete seemed to recover rather quickly. He was never one to be sickly and was proud of that. I remember one day when he was shooting staples from the air gun into the wall of our upstairs construction, one of those staples accidently went directly into the palm of his left hand below his thumb. He came down the stairs to show me what happened. After cleaning his hand with alcohol, he pulled out the staple right before my eyes. I thought I was going to faint! We always had a first aid kit around, so he took the sterile gauze and wrapped up his palm. I encouraged him this time to go to the ER to get a tetanus shot. Thankfully he did!

Because we heated our home with wood he had to look for large trees on our property to chop down, then cut all the branches and tree trunk into logs to fit into the woodstove. He enjoyed doing this over the years, even though we hired someone to deliver cords of wood as well. When he stacked the logs between trees near our building, I would take a few pictures. They looked so pretty stacked up neatly. They actually made a fence that kept the deer at bay, but the chipmunks and squirrels loved running in and out of the openings between the logs. This was a new home for the rabbits, too.

Pete was always excited when he had cut down a huge dead tree, usually ash or maple. This was good wood with an excellent R-value. The wood was dense and heavy — good for heating! The summer months after his heart attack, he decided to cut down a decayed dead 150-year-old ash tree located across the stream to the south. Fortunately, he had the right sized chain saw for the job. In fact, I believe he had five different size saws. This largest one would have been too heavy for one man to even grip, but because Pete was so muscular and strong, it was never a problem for him. Still, I always wanted him to have someone help with this tree chopping, but he wouldn't have it! He was quite proud and loved being able to do everything by himself.

He knew where to make the initial cuts in the lower trunk of the tree, so the tree would fall in the direction he wanted it to drop. His desire was to have it fall away from surrounding trees to avoid damaging them. He also knew where to tie heavy robes around that tree and surrounding trees as a brace for support during the fall. I always worried, but he was very careful. I knew of a friend's husband who died after trying to cut down a tree when it fell on top of him! So tragic!

After several days of cutting through the wide base of the trunk, Pete came back to the building eager to tell me the tree was down. The sound of the fall was very loud, so I knew when he had accomplished this monumental task! It looked huge laying there on the ground, but it would provide enough wood for the entire winter for us. We were happy for that. Now his task was to cut up the branches and the trunk of the tree. We didn't have a log splitter, so the task was colossal! Because of Pete's heart attack in late spring, I was concerned whether he could carry these heavy logs across the stream to our place. It was a project that would take several months, and I hoped he could finish this before the first frost. I didn't want him walking through the stream during the cold winter carrying a load of logs for fear he would slip in the icy stream and fall.

I noticed he wasn't short of breath while doing tasks, but I did notice his facial color seemed more ashen to me as the months progressed. I didn't want to worry him, but I was concerned about the function of his heart, even though he was taking his cardiac medication as prescribed by the cardiologists.

CHAPTER FORTY-NINE

One afternoon, Pete was standing where we cooked our meals in the small living quarters. I don't remember what he was doing at the time, but he suddenly turned to look my way. I was sitting at the foot of the bed, my designated seat, and with tears in his eyes he started to cry and say, "Bo, I am so sorry I didn't build that home you wanted."

I felt badly for him. His physical strength was his major pride, and he knew he was not as strong anymore. He was sixty-six years old now. The work required to finish the building was too much for him to accomplish alone, and he finally realized this. I tried to comfort him as best I could.

"I don't know how long I have left to live, and I don't want to go without you. We can go together; it would be painless really," he continued.

I knew what he meant by this last sentence, and it frightened me. We truly loved each other, despite all the problems we encountered along our journey. But suicide was not an answer for me.

My response was trite as I later thought about it, but it was appropriate for our situation, living the way we did all these years.

"I want to have a bathroom, a kitchen, and to feel carpet under my feet before I die. I'm not ready to go." I answered hesitantly.

Before waiting for his reply, something immediately came to my mind. One summer day a few years earlier we were concerned that I might have had a brain tumor. After getting all the tests, I returned home with the good news that I was okay. Pete came out of the building when he heard my car drive up. After I told him the positive results, he gave me a strong hug and kiss! He had tears in his eyes.

Whenever we were outside enjoying the nice warm weather, we sat on tree stumps that Pete carried back from the woods after felling a tree for our wood burning stove several years earlier. The stumps were our outdoor "chairs." We enjoyed the fragrances from the wildflowers, the gold finches feeding at a nearby birdfeeder, the squirrels and chipmunks running about, and just simply the beauty of our woods and listening to the rushing water from both streams. Our best conversations occurred while sitting side by side on those two stumps.

We slowly walked over and sat down on our two large tree stumps positioned against the south wall of our building in front of the three-car garage.

Feeling thankful for my report, Pete put his arm around me tightly, and said, "I would give up all these cars and all of my cherished possessions to keep you in my life, Bo. I can't live without you; my life would be miserable if I couldn't share it with you. You mean more to me than anything else."

Instead of giving him a kiss or hug, I simply replied, "That is how it is supposed to be!"

I got up from my tree stump and walked back into our living quarters. Thinking back to all the times when he became angry and showed mental and physical abuse prohibited me from showing any display of affection towards him. I don't know if he realized why I left him sitting there alone. Today though, I regret I didn't provide a loving comment or gesture.

Due to his diabetes, Pete was gradually losing his eyesight. As a craftsman, he needed to see well to do his work. I started to notice when he read articles, books, and manuals during the late evening hours, which he did almost every night, he started using a magnifying glass more and more often. He even moved his head lower to the page to get closer to the words in order to see better. He never complained about this. In fact, as I recall he never complained about anything. Nothing was a hardship for him. But I remember him saying that he prayed to God often to restore his eyesight when he noticed it was failing.

"I am an artist, Bo. I need my eyesight!" he would say sadly.

Watching him decline in body and spirit was difficult. Everything I loved about him was fading before my eyes. I wasn't sure what we were going to do. I couldn't take care of our property and cut wood to keep the place warm during winter. All the things Pete did, I couldn't do. I told him we needed to move away and find a finished house to live in comfortably for the rest of our lives.

We tried to sell the property a few years earlier, but no buyers were interested. With two streams, an unfinished 8000 sq. ft. building zoned for light industry, it didn't fit the needs of any prospective buyers. Our friend, whose father sold us the land, was our realtor. He felt Pete wanted too much for the place, so eventually we took it off the market.

I knew we were too old to continue living in the small quarters we called home, and I knew Pete couldn't continue with his car restoration business. So I too prayed for help and answers to our combined complicated problems.

CHAPTER FIFTY

One night after driving home through a few inches of new snow, I didn't see Pete waiting for me at our driveway entrance as he always did each night. He always wanted me to give him a call when I was about a mile from home, so he had time to walk down our road to the entrance where he waited for my approach. After stopping the car in the driveway, he would hop into the passenger seat. We would reach over and give each other a kiss before I slowly drove up the path to the building. This was our regular routine each night after I came home from work around 1:00 a.m.

The moon was full; the shadows cast from our sixty-foot trees were so pretty against the white ground. But as I slowly drove up our winding road, I became more concerned, wondering why Pete had not greeted me. When I reached the upper gate entrance, I noticed something moving near the ridge to the north about thirty yards away. It was Pete! He ran towards the car, and I waited as he approached.

He smiled and said, "Bo, I feel great! I just ran a little, and I don't feel tired or have any pain."

I was so relieved that he was all right and that he felt good! I knew this would be short lived, but I didn't want to discourage him, as I wanted him to feel hopeful, even with his cardiac condition. I wanted him to continue fulfilling his dream ambitions.

CHAPTER FIFTY-ONE

Pete loved taking that long walk down our pretty winding road to the entrance from the street. He did this walk even on my days off, and sometimes I would go with him. But each night around 1:00 o'clock in the morning there he was somewhere along that road. When there wasn't a moonlit sky, he took his flashlight with him. He loved the beauty of the night and listening to the sounds of the owls and nightingales. Often he said he took his deceased grandfather with him on these walks. He thought of him daily!

I was too tired this one particular night to go with him, so I went up the ladder and into my upper bunkbed to go to sleep. I had already retired from nursing due to a chronic illness of my own. I was sixty-two and wanted to work for several more years, but a hearing loss made that too difficult as well as other health issues.

"Bo, I'm going out now," he said as I covered myself up to get warm.

"Okay, I may be asleep by the time you return," I answered with a yawn.

I did hear Pete return about twenty minutes later, as he locked the outer doors of the garage and entered our small living space. He made some coffee as he always did and sat down in his chair.

Suddenly I heard a loud gasp! I raised up and leaned over the side of my upper bunk. Looking down I saw Pete sitting in the chair, his listless body slumped down with his head leaning to the left. There with some drooling from his mouth. As seen in movies, his coffee cup had fallen from his hand into his lap. I knew what had happened! I hurried down the ladder and after calling out his name several times, and getting no response, I did the cardiac thump over his heart! This attempt at jump starting patients' hearts when they had gone into VT (ventricular tachycardia) often was successful during my years of nursing. But, unfortunately, this did not work for Pete. I could not revive him! I kissed his forehead and cried profusely!

I was anticipating this eventually, but the reality of seeing him in this state was unbelievable. I know looking back that I was in shock! I immediately called one of Pete's friends who lived thirty miles away in a nearby town. Fortunately, like Pete, he was up during the late-night hours. He said he would drive down right away, and I felt comfort in that. It was about 3:00 in the morning and I had already called the medics. Pete's friend, Frank, arrived before the medics did. After Pete was pronounced dead by the medical team, I watched with almost disbelief as they carried him out of our place and into the ambulance.

My life with Pete was now a memory as were all the people I have mentioned that I didn't get to say goodbye to properly and satisfactorily.

EPILOGUE

I remember telling my brother, Jim, almost forty years earlier that I believed I was to help Pete learn a lesson in his life's journey. As I have mentioned, I would receive these cerebral messages over the course of my life. They seemed to guide me forward. Maybe that was how I endured our difficult marriage. Pete had to learn that material possessions did not equate to the love given and received from family and friends, as well as all personal contact. He finally realized this only months before his passing.

I believe we have a blueprint to follow in our life on this earth. We don't deviate from God's plan for us. The pathway for each of us is there to enrich our lives before our journey is complete.

I am saddened by not being able to have expressed my love sufficiently to each of the individuals in my life who passed away. But I believe this is part of my blueprint. These wrong goodbyes are part of my journey.

With lots of tears coming from both Cyndi and I, we pack up the picnic supplies. Neither of us expressed any further comment. She gave me a strong hug and wheeled me back to my room.

www.ingramcontent.com/pod-product-compliance
Lightning Source LLC
LaVergne TN
LVHW011934070526
838202LV00054B/4640